STEVE AND THE STEAM ENGINE

Also by Sara Ware Bassett

<table>
<tr><td>THE YOUNG ENGINEERS</td><td>THE STORY OF</td></tr>
<tr><td>Carl and the Cotton Gin</td><td>The Story of Glass</td></tr>
<tr><td>Christopher and the
    Clockmakers</td><td>The Story of Leather</td></tr>
<tr><td></td><td>The Story of Silk</td></tr>
<tr><td>Paul and the Printing Press</td><td>The Story of Sugar</td></tr>
<tr><td>Steve and the Steam Engine</td><td>The Story of Porcelain</td></tr>
<tr><td>Ted and the Telephone</td><td>The Story of Lumber</td></tr>
<tr><td>Walter and the Wireless</td><td>The Story of Wool</td></tr>
</table>

Find these and hundreds of more great books at
www.livingbookpress.com

This edition published 2026
by Living Book Press

ISBN: 978-1-76153-461-4 (hardcover)
           978-1-76153-469-0 (softcover)

First published in 1921.

This edition is based on the Little, Brown, and Company printing by 1921.

A catalogue record for this
book is available from the
National Library of Australia

STEVE AND THE STEAM ENGINE

by

SARA WARE BASSETT

"IT WAS THE CONQUERING OF THIS MULTITUDE OF DEFECTS THAT GAVE
TO THE WORLD THE INTRICATE, EXQUISITELY MADE MACHINE."

Contents

CHAPTER I

AN UNPREMEDITATED FOLLY

Steve Tolman had done a wrong thing and he knew it.

While his father, mother, and sister Doris had been absent in New York for a week-end visit and Havens, the chauffeur, was ill at the hospital, the boy had taken the big six-cylinder car from the garage without anybody's permission and carried a crowd of his friends to Torrington to a football game. And that was not the worst of it, either. At the foot of the long hill leading into the village the mighty leviathan so unceremoniously borrowed had come to a halt, refusing to move another inch, and Stephen now sat helplessly in it, awaiting the aid his comrades had promised to send back from the town.

What an ignominious climax to what had promised to be a royal holiday! Steve scowled with chagrin and disappointment.

The catastrophe served him right. Unquestionably he should not have taken the car without asking. He had never run it all by himself before, although many times he had driven it when either his father or Havens had been at his elbow. It had gone all right then. What reason had he to suppose a mishap would befall him when they were not by? It was infernally hard luck!

Goodness only knew what was the matter with the thing. Probably something was smashed, something that might require days or even weeks to repair, and would cost a lot of money. Here was a pretty dilemma!

How angry his father would be!

The family were going to use the automobile Saturday to take Doris back to Northampton for the opening of college and had planned to make quite a holiday of the trip. Now it would all have to be given up and everybody would blame him for the disappointment. A wretched hole he was in!

The boys had not given him much sympathy, either. They had been ready enough to egg him on into wrong-doing and had made of the adventure the jolliest lark imaginable; but the moment fun had been transformed into calamity they had deserted him with incredible speed, climbing out of the spacious tonneau and trooping jauntily off on foot to see the town. It was easy enough for them to wash their hands of the affair and leave him to the solitude of the roadside; the automobile was not theirs and when they got home they would not be confronted by irate parents.

How persuasively, reflected Stephen, they had urged him on.

"Oh, be a sport, Steve!" Jack Curtis had coaxed. "Who's going to be the wiser if you do take the car? Anyhow, you have run it before, haven't you? I don't believe your father will mind."

"Take a chance, Stevie," his chum, Bud Taylor, pleaded. "What's the good of being such a boob? Do you think if my father had a car and it was standing idle in the garage when a bunch of kids needed it to go to a school game I would hesitate? You bet I wouldn't!"

"It isn't likely your Dad would balk at your using the car if he knew the circumstances," piped another boy. "We have got that match to play off, and now that the electric cars are held up by the strike how are we to get to Torrington? Don't be a ninny, Steve."

Thus they had ridiculed, cajoled, and wheedled Steve until his conscience had been overpowered and, yielding to their arguments, he had set forth for the adjoining village with the triumphant throng of tempters. At first all had gone well. The fourteen miles had slipped past with such smoothness and rapidity that Stephen, proudly enthroned at the wheel, had almost forgotten that any shadow rested on the hilarity of the day. He had been dubbed a good fellow, a true sport, a benefactor to the school—every complimentary pseudonym imaginable—and had glowed with pleasure beneath the avalanche of flattery. As the big car with its rollicking occupants had spun along the highway, many a passer-by had caught the merry mood of the cheering group and waved a smiling salutation in response to their shouts.

In the meanwhile, exhilarated by the novelty of the escapade, Steve had increased the speed until the red car fairly shot over the level macadam, its blurred outlines lost in the scarlet of the autumn foliage. Then suddenly when the last half-mile was reached and Torrington village, the goal of the pilgrimage, was in sight, quite without warning the panting monster had stopped and all attempts to urge it farther were of no avail. There it stood, its motionless engine sending out odors of hot varnish and little shimmering waves of heat.

Immediately a hush had descended upon the boisterous company. There was a momentary pause, followed by a clamor of advice. When, however, it became evident that there was no prospect of restoring the disabled machine to action, one after another of the frightened schoolboys had dropped out over the sides of the car and after loitering an instant or two with a sort of shamefaced indecision, at the suggestion of Bud Taylor they had all set out for the town.

"Tough luck, old chap!" Bud had called over his shoulder. "Mighty tough luck! Wish we had time to wait and see what's queered the thing; but the game is called at two-thirty, you know, and we have only about time to make it. We'll try and hunt up a garage and send somebody back to help you. So long!"

And away they had trooped without so much as a backward glance, leaving Stephen alone on the country road, worried, mortified, and resentful. There was no excuse for their heartless conduct, he fumed indignantly. They were not all on the eleven. Five of the team had come over in Tim Barclay's Ford, so that several of the fellows Steve had brought were merely to be spectators of the game. At least Bud Taylor, his especial crony, was not playing. He might have remained behind. How selfish people were, and what a fleeting thing was popularity! Why, half an hour ago he had been the idol of the crowd! Then Bud had shouted: "Come ahead, kids, let's hoof it to Torrington!" and in the twinkling of an eye the tide had turned, the mob had shifted its allegiance and gone tagging off at the heels of a new leader. They did not mean to have their pleasure spoiled, not they!

Scornfully Stephen watched them mount the hill, their crimson sweaters making a zigzag line of color in the sunshine; even their laughter, care-free as if nothing had happened, floated back to him on the still air, demonstrating how little concern they felt for him and his refractory automobile. Well might they proceed light-heartedly to the village, spend their money on sodas and ice-cream cones, and shout themselves hoarse at the game. No thought of future punishment marred their enjoyment and the program was precisely the one he had outlined for himself before Fate had intervened and raised a prohibitory hand.

The fun he had missed was, however, of scant consequence now. All he asked was to get the car safely back to his father's garage before the family returned from New York on the afternoon train. Now that his excitement had cooled into sober second thought, he marveled that he had been led into committing such a monstrous offense. He must have been mad. Often he had begged to do the very thing he had done and his father had always refused to let him, insisting that an expensive touring car was no toy for a boy of his age. Perhaps there had been some truth in the assertion, too, he now admitted. Yet were he to hang for it, he could not see why he had not run the car exactly as his elders were wont to do. Of course he had had a pretty big crowd aboard and the heavy load might have strained the machinery; and possibly—just possibly—he had speeded a bit. He certainly had made phenomenally good time for he did not want the fellows to think he was afraid to let out the engine.

Well, whatever the matter was, the harm was done now and he was in a most unenviable plight. No doubt it would cost a small fortune to get the automobile into shape again, more money than he had in the world; certainly far more than he had in his pocket at the present moment. What was he to do? Even suppose the boys did remember to send back help (they probably wouldn't—but suppose they did) how was he to pay a machinist? As he pictured himself being towed to a garage and the car being left there, he felt an uncomfortable sensation in his throat. He certainly was in for it now.

It would be ignominious to charge the repairs to his father but that would be the only course left him. Fortunately Mr. Tolman, who was a railroad official, was well known in the locality and therefore there would be no trouble about obtaining credit; but to ask his father to pay the bills for this escapade was anything but a manly and honorable way out and Steve wished with all his heart he had never been persuaded into the wretched affair. If there were only some escape possible, some alternative from being obliged to confess his wrong-doing! But to hope to conceal or make good the disaster was futile. And even if he could cover up what had happened, how contemptible it would be! He detested doing anything underhanded. Only sneaks and cowards resorted to subterfuge and although he had been called many names in his life these two had not been among them.

No, he should make a clean breast of what he had done and bear the consequences, and once out of his miserable plight he would take care never again to be a party to such an adventure. He had learned his lesson.

So absorbed was he in framing these worthy resolutions that he did not notice a tiny moving speck that appeared above the crest of the hill and now came whirling toward him. In fact the dusty truck and its yet more dusty driver were beside him before he heeded either one. Then the newcomer came to a stop and he heard a pleasant voice:

"What's the matter, sonny?"

Stephen glanced up, trying bravely to return his questioner's smile.

The man who addressed him was white-haired, ruddy, and muscular, and he wore brown denim overalls stained with oil and grease; but although he was middle-aged there was a boyish friendliness in his face and in the frank blue eyes that peered out from under his shaggy brows.

"What's the trouble with your machine?" he repeated.

"I don't know," returned Stephen. "If I did, you bet I wouldn't be sitting here."

The workman laughed.

"You've got your engine nicely warmed up, youngster," he observed casually.

"Suppose you let me have a look at it," said he, climbing off the seat on which he was perched.

"I wish you would."

"It is a pretty fine car, isn't it?" observed the man, as he approached it. "Is it yours?"

"My father's."

"He lets you use it, eh?"

Stephen did not answer.

"Some fathers ain't that generous," went on the man as he began to examine the silent monster. "If I had an outfit like this, I ain't so sure I'd trust it to a chap of your size. Still, if you have your license, I suppose you must know how to run it."

A shiver passed through Stephen's body. A license! What if the stranger should ask to see it?

There was a heavy fine, he now remembered, for driving a car unless one were in possession of this precious paper, although what the penalty was he could not at the instant recall; he had entirely forgotten there were any such legal details. Fearfully he eyed the mechanic.

The man, however, did not pursue the subject but instead appeared engrossed in carefully inspecting the automobile inside and out. As he poked about, now here, now there, Stephen watched him with constantly increasing nervousness; and after the investigation had proceeded for some little time and no satisfactory result had been reached, the boy's heart sank. Something very serious must be the matter if the trouble were so hard to locate, he reasoned. In imagination he heard his father's indignant reprimands and saw the Northampton trip shrivel into nothingness.

The workman in the meantime remained silent, offering no comment to relieve his anxiety. What he was thinking under the shabby visor cap pulled so low over his brows it was impossible to fathom. His hand was now unscrewing the top of the gasoline tank.

"You've got your engine nicely warmed up, youngster," observed he casually. "Maybe 'twas just as well you did come to a stop. You must have covered the ground at a pretty good clip."

There certainly was something very disconcerting about the stranger's conversation and again Stephen looked at him with suspicion.

"Oh, I don't know," he mumbled, trying to assume an off-hand air. "Perhaps we did come along fairly fast."

"You weren't alone then."

"N—o," was the uncomfortable reply. "The fellows who sent you back from the village were with me."

For the first time the workman evinced surprise.

"Nobody sent me," he retorted. "I just thought as I was going by that you looked as if you were up against it, and as I happen to know something about engines I pulled up to give you a helping hand. The fix you are in isn't serious, though." He smiled broadly as if something amused him.

"What is the matter with the car?" demanded the boy desperately, in a voice that trembled with eagerness and anxiety and defied all efforts to remain under his control.

"Why, son, nothing is wrong with your car. You've got no gasoline, that's all."

"Gasoline!" repeated the lad blankly.

"Sure! You couldn't have had much aboard when you started, I guess. It managed to bring you as far as this, however, and here you came to a stop. The up-grade of the hill tipped the little gas you did have back in the tank so it would not run out, you see. Fill her up again and she'll sprint along as nicely as ever."

The relief that came with the information almost bowled Steve over.

For a moment he could not speak; then when he had caught his breath he exclaimed excitedly:

"How can I get some gasoline?"

His rescuer laughed at the fevered question.

"Why, I happen to have a can of it here on my truck," he drawled, "and I can let you have part of it if you are so minded."

"Oh, I don't want to take yours," objected the boy.

"Nonsense! Why not? I am going right past a garage on my way back and can get plenty more. We'll tip enough of mine into your tank to carry you home. It won't take a minute."

The suggestion was like water to the thirsty.

"All right!" cried Stephen. "If you will let me pay for it I shall be mightily obliged to you. I'm mightily obliged anyway."

"Pshaw! I've done nothing," protested the person in the oily jumper. "What are we in the world for if not to do one another a good turn when we can?"

As he spoke he extricated from his conglomerate load of lumber, tools, and boxes a battered can, the contents of which he began to transfer into Stephen's empty tank.

"There!" ejaculated he presently, as he screwed the metal top on. "That isn't all she'll hold, but it will at least get you home. You are going right back, aren't you?"

The boy glanced quickly at the speaker.

"Yes."

"That's right. I would if I were in your place," urged the man.

Furtively Stephen scrutinized the countenance opposite but although the words had contained a mingled caution and rebuke there was not the slightest trace of interest in the face of the speaker, who was imperturbably wiping off the moist nickel cap with a handful of waste from his pocket.

"Yes," he repeated half-absently, "I take it that amount of gas will just about carry you back to Coventry; it won't allow for any detours, to be sure, but if you follow the straight road it ought to fetch you up there all right."

Stephen started and again an interrogation rose to his lips. Who was this mysterious mechanic and why should he assume with such certainty that Coventry was the abiding place of the car? He longed to ask but a fear of lengthening the interview prevented him from doing so. If he began to ask questions might not the stranger assume the same privilege and wheel upon him with some embarrassing inquiry? No, the sooner he was clear of this wizard in the brown overalls the better. But for the sake of his peace of mind he should like to know whether the man really knew who he was or whether his comments were simply matters of chance. There certainly was something very uncanny and uncomfortable about it all, something that led him to feel that the person in the jumper was fully acquainted with his escapade, disapproved of it, and meant to prevent him from prolonging it. Yet as he took a peep into the kindly blue eyes which he did not trust himself to meet directly he wondered if this assumption were not created by a guilty conscience rather than by fact. Certainly there was nothing accusatory in the other's bearing. His face was frankness itself. In books criminals were always fearing that people suspected them, reflected Steve. The man knew nothing about him at all. It was absurd to think he did.

Nevertheless the boy was eager to be gone from the presence of those searching blue eyes and therefore he climbed into his car, murmuring hurriedly:

"You've been corking to help me out!"

The workman held up a protesting hand.

"Don't think of it again," he answered. "I was glad to do it. Good luck to you!"

With nervous hands Stephen started the engine and, backing the automobile about, headed it homeward. Now that danger was past his desire to reach Coventry before his father should arrive drove every other thought from his mind, and soon the mysterious hero of the brown jumper was forgotten. Although he made wonderfully good time back over the road it seemed hours before he turned in at his own gate and brought the throbbing motor to rest in the garage. A sigh of thankfulness welled up within him. The great red leviathan that had caused him such anguish of spirit stood there in the stillness as peacefully as if it had never stirred from the spot it occupied. If only it had remained there, how glad the boy would have been.

He ventured to look toward the windows fronting the avenue. No one was in sight, it was true; but to flatter himself that he had been unobserved was ridiculous for he saw by the clock that his father, mother, and Doris must already have reached home. Doubtless they were in the house now and fully acquainted with what he had done. If they had not missed the car from the garage they would at least have seen it whirl into the driveway with him at the wheel. Any moment his father might appear at his shoulder. To delay was useless. He had had his fun and now in manly fashion he must face the music and pay for it. How he dreaded the coming storm!

Once, twice he braced himself, then moved reluctantly toward the house, climbed the steps, and let himself in at the front door. He could hardly expect any one would come to greet him under the circumstances. An ominous silence pervaded the great dim hall but after the glare of the white ribbon of road on which his eyes had been so intently fixed he found the darkness cool and tranquilizing. At first he could scarcely see; then as he gradually became accustomed to the faint light he espied on the silver card tray a telegram addressed to himself and with a quiver of apprehension tore it open. Telegrams were not such a common occurrence in his life that he had ceased to regard them with misgiving.

The message on which his gaze rested, however, contained no ill tidings. On the contrary it merely announced that the family had been detained in New York longer than they had expected and would not return until noon to-morrow. He would have almost another day, therefore, before he would be forced to make confession to his father! The respite was a welcome one and with it his tenseness relaxed. He even gained courage on the strength of his steadier nerves to creep into the kitchen and confront Mary, the cook, whom he knew must have seen him shoot into the driveway and who, having been years in the home, would not hesitate to lecture him roundly for his conduct. But Mary was not there and neither was Julia, the waitress. In the absence of the head of the house the two had evidently ascended to the third story there to forget in sleep the cares of daily life. Stephen smiled at the discovery. It was a coincidence. Unquestionably Fate was with him. It helped his self-respect to feel that at least the servants were in ignorance of what he had done. Nobody knew—nobody at all!

With an interval of rest and a dash of cold water upon his face gradually the act he had committed began to sink back into normal perspective and loom less gigantic in his memory. After all was it such a dreadful thing, he asked himself. Of course he should not have done it and he fully intended to confess his fault and accept the blame. But was the folly so terrible? He owned that he regretted it and admitted that he was somewhat troubled over the probable consequences, and every time he awoke in the night a dread of the morrow came upon him. In the morning he rushed off to school, found the team had won the game, and came home feeling even more justified than before. Why, if he had not taken the car, the school might have forfeited that victory!

All the afternoon as he sat quietly at his books he tried to keep this consideration uppermost in his mind. Then at dinner time there was a stir in the hall and he knew the moment he feared had arrived. The family were back again! Slowly he stole down over the heavily carpeted stairs. Yes, there they were, just coming in at the door, laughing and chatting gaily with Julia, who had let them in. The next instant his mother had espied him on the landing and had called a greeting.

There was a smile on her face that reproached him for having yielded to the temptation to deceive her even for a second.

"Such a delightful trip as we have had, Steve!" she called. "We wished a dozen times that you were with us. But some vacation you shall have a holiday in New York with your father to pay for what you have missed this time. You shall not be cheated out of all the fun, dear boy!"

"Everything been all right here, son?" inquired his father from the foot of the stairs.

"Yes, Dad."

"Havens has not showed up yet, I suppose."

The boy flushed.

"No, sir."

"It seems to take him an interminable time to have his tonsils out. If he does not appear pretty soon I shall have to get another man to run the car. We can't be left high and dry like this," fretted the elder man irritably. "Suppose I knew nothing about it, where would we be? I wished to-day you were old enough to have a license and could have come to the station to meet us. I believe with a little more instruction you could manage that automobile all right. Not that I should let you go racing over the country with a lot of boys. But you might be very useful in taking your mother and sister about and helping when we were in a fix like this. I think you would enjoy doing it, too."

"I—I'm—sure I should," replied the lad, avoiding his father's eye and studying the toe of his shoe intently. It passed through his mind as he stood there that now was the moment for confession. He had only to say,

"*I had the car out yesterday,*" and the dreaded ordeal would be over. But somehow he could not utter the words. Instead he descended from the landing and followed the others into the library where the conversation immediately shifted to other topics. In the jumble of narrative his chance to speak was swallowed up nor during the next few days did any suitable opportunity occur for him to make his belated confession. When Mr. Tolman was not at meetings of the railroad board he was at his office or occupied with important affairs, and by and by so many events had intervened that to go back into the past seemed to Stephen idle sentimentality. At length he had lulled his conscience into deciding that in view of the conditions it was quite unnecessary to acquaint his father and mother with his wrong-doing at all. He was safely out of the entanglement and was it not just as well to accept his escape with gratitude and let sleeping dogs lie? All the punishments in the world could not change anything now. What would be the use of telling?

CHAPTER II

A MEETING WITH AN OLD FRIEND

The day of the excursion to Northampton was one of those clear mornings when a light frost turned the maples to vermilion and in a single night transformed the ripening summer foliage to the splendor of autumn. The Tolman family were in the highest spirits; it was not often that Mr. Tolman could be persuaded to leave his business and steal away for a week-end and when he did it was always a cause for great rejoicing. Doris, elated at the prospect of rejoining her college friends, was also in the happiest frame of mind and tripped up and down stairs, collecting her forgotten possessions and jamming them into her already bulging suitcase.

As for Steve, the prickings of conscience that had at first tormented him and made him shrink from being left alone with his father had quite vanished. He had argued himself into a state of mental tranquility where further punishment for his misdemeanor seemed superfluous. After his hairbreadth escape from disaster there was no danger, he argued, of his repeating the experiment, and was not this the very lesson all punishments sought to instill? If he had achieved this result without bothering his father about the details, why so much the better. Did not the old adage say that "experience is the best teacher"? Certainly in this case the maxim held true.

Having thus excused his under-handedness and stifled the protests of his better nature he felt, or tried to feel, entirely at peace with the world; and as he now sauntered out to greet the new day he did it as jauntily as if he had nothing to conceal. Already the car was at the door with the luggage aboard and its engine humming invitingly. As the boy listened to the sound he could not but rejoice that the purring monster could tell no tales. How disconcerting it would be should the scarlet devil suddenly shout aloud: "Well, Steve, don't you hope we do not get stalled to-day the way we did going to Torrington?" Mercifully there was no danger of that. The engine might puff and purr and snort but at least it could not talk, and his secret was quite safe. This reflection lighted his face with courage and when the family came out to join him no one would have suspected that the slender boy waiting on the doorstep harbored a thought of anything but anticipation in the prospect of the coming holiday.

"Is everything in, Steve?" asked his father, approaching with Doris's remaining grip.

"I think so, Dad," was the reply. "It certainly seems as if I had piled in almost a dozen suitcases."

"Nonsense, Stevie," pouted Doris. "There were only four."

"Five, Miss Sophomore!" contradicted her brother. "Five! That one Dad is bringing makes the fifth, and I would be willing to bet that it is yours."

"That's where you are wrong, Smartie," the girl laughed good-humoredly, making a mischievous grimace at him from beneath the brim of her saucy little toque of blue velvet. "I am not guilty of the extra suitcase. It's mother's."

"Your mother's!" ejaculated Mr. Tolman incredulously. "Mercy on us! I never knew your mother to be starting out on a short trip with such an array of gowns." Then turning toward his wife, he added in bantering fashion: "Aren't you getting a little frivolous, my dear? If it were Doris now—"

"But it isn't this time!" interrupted the young lady triumphantly.

Her mother exchanged a glance with her and they both laughed.

"No, Henry, I am the one to blame," Mrs. Tolman admitted. "You see, if I am to keep pace with my big son and daughter I must look my best; so I have not only brought the extra suitcase but I am going to be tremendously fussy as to where it is put."

"I do believe Mater's brought all her jewels with her!" Steve declared wickedly. "Well, she shall have her sunbursts, tiaras, and things where she can keep her eye on them every moment. Suppose I put them down here at your feet, Mother."

Without further ado, he started to lift the basket suitcase into the car.

"Don't tip it up, son. Don't tip it up!" cautioned his mother.

"Your mother is afraid of knocking some of the pearls or emeralds out of their setting," chuckled Mr. Tolman. "Go easy, Steve!"

A general laugh arose as the offending piece of baggage was stowed away out of sight. An instant later wraps and rugs were bundled in, everybody was cosily tucked up, and Mr. Tolman placed his hands on the wheel.

"Now we're off, Dad!" cried Stephen, as he sprang in beside his father. Mr. Tolman needed no second bidding.

There was a whir, a leap forward, and the automobile glided down the long avenue and out into the highway.

Steve, studying the road map, was too much interested in tracing out the route they were to follow to notice that after the car had spun along smoothly for several miles its speed lessened, and it was not until it came to a complete standstill that he aroused himself from his preoccupation sufficiently to see that his father was bending forward over the starter.

"What's wrong, Henry?" inquired his wife from the back seat.

"I can't imagine," was the impatient reply. "Had I not left the tank with gasoline in it, I should say it was empty; but of course that cannot be the case, for I always keep enough in it to carry us to the garage. Otherwise we should be stalled at our own doorstep and not able to get anywhere."

Climbing out, he began to unscrew the metal top of the tank while Stephen watched him in consternation.

The boy did not need to hear the result of the investigation for already the wretched truth flashed upon him. The tank was empty; of course it was! He knew that without being told. Had not the workman who had replenished it Wednesday said quite plainly that there was only enough gas in it to get him home to Coventry? He should have remembered to stop at the garage and take on an extra supply on the way back as his father always did. How stupid he had been! In his haste to get home he had forgotten every other consideration and the present dilemma was the result of his thoughtlessness. Yet how could he have stopped at the Coventry garage even had he thought of it? All the men there knew him and his father, and if he had gone there or had even driven through the center of the town somebody would have been sure to see him and mention the incident. Why, it was to avoid this very danger that he had returned by the less frequented way.

The man in the brown jeans had certainly calculated to a nicety when he measured out that gasoline. He had not meant him to do any more riding that day; that was apparent. What business was it of his, anyway, and why was he so solicitous as to where he went? There was something puzzling about that man. Steve had thought so at the time. Not that it mattered now. All that did matter was that here they were stalled at the side of the road in almost the same spot where he had been stalled the other day; and they were there because he had neglected to procure gasoline.

The lad felt the hot blood throb in his cheeks. Again the chance for confession confronted him and again his tongue was tied. In a word he could have explained the whole predicament; but he did not. Instead he sat as if stunned, the heart inside him pounding violently. He saw that his father was not only deeply annoyed but baffled to solve the incident.

"The gas is all out; that's the trouble!" he announced.

"What are we going to do, Dad?" inquired Doris anxiously.

"Oh, we can get more all right, daughter," returned her father reassuringly. "Don't worry, my dear. But what I can't understand is how we come to be in such a plight."

"Doesn't gasoline evaporate, Henry?" suggested Mrs. Tolman.

"To some extent, yes; but there could be no such shrinkage as this unless there was a leak in the tank. I never dreamed the supply was so low. Well, it is my own fault. I should have made sure everything was right before we started."

Steve shifted his position uncomfortably. He was manly enough not to enjoy hearing his father shoulder blame that did not rightfully belong to him.

"Now let me think what we had better do," went on Mr. Tolman. "Unfortunately there isn't a house in sight from which we can telephone for help; and we are fully five miles from Torrington. Our only hope is that some one bound for the town may overtake us and allow Steve to ride to the village for aid."

"Couldn't I walk it, Dad?" asked the boy, with an impulse to make good the mischief he had done.

"Oh, no; I wouldn't do that unless the worst befalls," his father replied kindly. "We should gain nothing. It is a long tramp and would simply be a waste of time. Let us wait like Mr. Micawber, and see if something does not turn up."

Wretchedly Stephen settled back into his seat. He would rather have walked to Torrington, done almost anything rather than remain there in the quiet autumn stillness and listen to the accusations of his conscience. What a coward he was!

"It is a shame for us to be tied up here!" he heard Doris complain.

"I know it, daughter, and I am as sorry as you are," responded her father patiently. "In fact, probably, I am more sorry, since it is through my own carelessness that we are stranded."

Again the impulse to blurt out the truth and take the blame that belonged to him took possession of Stephen; but with resolution he forced it back. Nervously he fingered the road map. If he had only spoken at the beginning! It was harder now. He should have made a clean breast of the whole affair when his father got home from New York. Then was the time to have done it. But since he had let that opportunity pass it was awkward, almost absurd, to make confession now. He would much better keep still.

In the meanwhile a gradual depression fell upon the occupants of the car. Mrs. Tolman did not speak; Doris subsided into hushed annoyance; and Mr. Tolman began to pace back and forth at the side of the road and anxiously scan the stretch of macadam that narrowed away between the avenue of trees bordering the highway. Presently he uttered an exclamation of relief.

"Here comes a truck!" he cried. "We will tip the driver and persuade him to let you ride on to Torrington with him, Steve. This is great luck!"

Stepping into the pathway of the approaching car he held up his hand and the passer-by came to a stop beside him.

Stephen looked up expectantly; then a thrill of foreboding seized him and he quickly turned his head aside. It needed no second glance to assure him that the man whom his father was addressing was none other than the workman in the brown jeans who had rescued him from his former plight. He bent lower over the road map, trying to conceal his face and decide what to do. In another moment the teamster would probably recognize him, recall the incident of their former meeting, and hailing him as an old acquaintance, relate the entire story. The possibility was appalling, but terrible as it was it did not equal the disquietude he experienced when he heard his father ejaculate with sudden surprise:

"Why, if it isn't O'Malley! I did not recognize you, Jake. You are just in time to extricate us from a most inconvenient situation. We are headed for Northampton and find ourselves without gasoline. If you can take my son along to Torrington with you so he can hunt up a garage and ride back with some one on a service car I shall be very grateful to you."

"I'd be glad to go myself, sir."

"No, no! I shall not allow you to do that," protested Mr. Tolman. "You are on your way to work and I could not think of detaining you. All I ask is that you take my boy along to the village."

"I'd really be pleased to go, sir," reiterated O'Malley. "I am in no great rush."

"No, I shan't hear to it, Jake," Mr. Tolman repeated. "Nevertheless I appreciate your offer. Take the boy along and that is all I'll ask. Come, Steve, jump aboard! O'Malley, son, is one of our railroad people, whose services we value highly. He is going to be good enough to let you ride over to Torrington with him."

Although the introduction compelled Stephen to give the waiting employee a nod of greeting, he did not meet his eye or evince any sign of recognition, and he sensed that the light that had flashed into the man's face at sight of him died out as quickly as it had come. The boy had an uncomfortable realization as he climbed to the seat of the truck and took his place beside its driver that O'Malley must be rating him as a snob. No one but a cad would accept a stranger's kindness and then cut him dead the next time he encountered him. It was better to endure this misjudgment, however, than to acknowledge a previous acquaintance with the mechanic and thereby arouse his father's suspicion and curiosity. Hence, without further parley, he settled himself and in silence the truck started off.

For some minutes he waited, expecting that when they were well out of earshot of the family the man at the wheel would turn and with a laugh make some reference to the adventure of the past week. It certainly must have amused him to find the great red car again stalled in the same spot, and what would be more natural than that he should comment on the coincidence and perhaps make a joke of the circumstance? But to the boy's chagrin the teamster did no such thing. Instead he kept his eyes fixed on the road and gave no evidence that he had ever before seen the lad at his elbow.

Stephen was aghast. It was not possible the workman had forgotten the happening. He began to feel very uncomfortable. As the landscape slipped past and the car sped on, the distance to Torrington lessened. Still there seemed to be no prospect of the stranger at the wheel breaking his silence. If it had merely been a silence perhaps Steve would not have minded so much; but there was an implied rebuke in the stillness that nettled and stung and left him with a consciousness of being ignored by a superior being.

"I say!" he burst out, when he could endure the ignominy of his position no longer, "don't you remember me, Mr. O'Malley?"

The man who guided the car did not turn his head but he nodded.

"I remember you all right," replied he politely. "I just thought you did not remember me."

"Oh, I remembered you right away," declared Steve eagerly.

"Did you?"

There was a subtle irony in the tone that the lad was not clever enough to detect.

"Of course."

"Is that so!" came dryly from O'Malley.

"Yes, indeed! I remembered you right away," Steve stumbled on. "You are the man who gave me the gasoline when I was stuck here Wednesday."

"I am."

"I knew you the first minute I saw you," repeated Stephen.

"I did not notice any sign that you did," was the terse response.

"Oh—well—you see, I couldn't very well speak back there," explained Steve with confusion. "They would all have wanted to know where I—I mean I would have to—it would just have made a lot of talk," concluded he lamely.

For the first time the elder man, moving his eyes from the ribbon of gleaming highway, confronted him.

"So your father did not know you had the car out the other day?" said he.

"N—o."

The workman showed no surprise.

"I guessed as much," he remarked. "But of course you have told him since."

"Not yet," Steve stammered. "I was going to—honest I was; but things kept interrupting until it got to be so late that it seemed silly to rake the matter all up. Besides, I shan't do it again, so what is the use of jawing about it?"

He stopped, awaiting a response from the railroad employee; but none came.

"Anyhow," he argued with rising irritability, "what good does it do to discuss things that are over and done with? You can't undo them."

The man at the wheel vouchsafed no answer.

"It is because I forgot to stop for more gas when I went home the other day that we are in this fix now," Steve finally blurted out, finding relief in brutal confession.

Still the only reply to his monologue was the chugging of the engine.

At last his voice rose to a higher pitch and there was anger in it.

"I'm talking to you," he shouted in exasperation.

"I am listening."

"Well, why don't you say something?"

"What is there to say?"

"Why—eh—you could tell me what you think."

"I guess you know that already."

Stephen's face turned scarlet.

"I did intend to tell my father," repeated he, instantly on the defensive. "Straight goods, I did."

The man shrugged his shoulders.

"It was only that it didn't seem to come right. You know how things go sometimes."

He saw the workman's lip curl.

"You think I ought to have told."

"Have I said so?"

"No, but I know you do think so."

"I wasn't aware I'd expressed any opinion."

"No—but—well—hang it all—you think I am a coward for not making a clean breast of the whole thing!" cried Stephen, now thoroughly enraged.

"What do you think yourself?" O'Malley suddenly inquired with disconcerting directness.

"Oh, I know I've been rotten," admitted the boy. "Still, even now—" He paused.

"You mean that even now it isn't too late?" put in the truckman, his face lighting to a smile.

"N—o; that wasn't exactly what I was going to say," began the lad, resuming his argumentative tone. "What I mean is that—"

A swift frown replaced the elder man's smile.

"Here we are at the garage," he broke in. "They will do whatever you want them to."

He seemed in a hurry and as Stephen could find no excuse for lingering he climbed reluctantly out of the truck and stood balancing himself on the curb that edged the sidewalk.

"I'm much obliged to you for bringing me over," he observed awkwardly.

"That's all right."

The man in the brown jeans started his engine.

"Say, Mr. O'Malley!" called Stephen desperately.

"Well?"

"You—you—won't tell my father about my taking the car, will you?" he pleaded wretchedly.

"*I* tell him?"

Never had he heard so much scorn compressed into three words.

"You need have no worries," declared the man over his shoulder, a contemptuous sneer curling his lips. "I confess my own wrong-doing but I do not tattle the sins of other people. Your father will never be the wiser about you so far as I am concerned. Whatever you want him to know you will have to tell him yourself."

Baffled, mortified, and stinging with humiliation as if he had been whipped, Stephen watched him disappear round the bend of the road.

O'Malley despised him, that he knew; and he did not at all relish being despised.

CHAPTER III

A SECOND CALAMITY

While hunting up the garage and negotiating for gasoline Steve thrust resolutely from his mind his encounter with O'Malley and the galling sense of inferiority it carried with it; but once on the highroad again the smart returned and the sting lingering behind the man's scorn was not to be allayed. It required every excuse his wounded dignity could muster to bolster up his pride and make out for himself the plausible case that had previously comforted him and lulled his conscience to rest. It was now more impossible than ever for him to make any confession, he decided; for having denied in his father's presence O'Malley's acquaintance it would be ridiculous to acknowledge that he had known the truck driver all along. Of course he could not do that. Whatever he might have said or done at the time, it was entirely too late to go back on his conduct now. One event had followed on the heels of another until to slip out a single stone of the structure he had built up would topple over the whole house.

If he had spoken in the beginning that would have been quite simple. All he could do now was to let bygones be bygones and in the pleasure of to-day forget the mistakes of yesterday. Consoled by this reflection he managed to recapture such a degree of his self-esteem that by the time he rejoined the family he was once more holding his head in the air and smiling with his wonted lightness of heart.

"We shall get you to Northampton now, daughter, without more delay, I hope," Mrs. Tolman affirmed when the car was again skimming along. "We may be a bit behind schedule; nevertheless a late arrival by motor will be pleasanter than to have made the trip by train."

"I should say so!" was the fervent ejaculation.

"Come, come!" interrupted Mr. Tolman. "I shall not sit back and allow you two people to cry down the railroads. They are not perfect, I will admit, and unquestionably trains do not always go at the hours we wish they did; a touring car is, perhaps, a more comfortable and luxurious method of travel, especially in summer. But just as it is an improvement over the train, so the train was a mighty advance over the stagecoach of olden days."

"Oh, I don't know, Dad," Stephen mused. "I am not so sure that I should not have liked stagecoaches better. Think what jolly sport it must have been to drive all over the country!"

"In fine weather, yes—that is, if the roads had been as excellent as they are now; but you must remember that in the old coaching days road-building had not reached its present perfection. Traveling by stage over a rough highway in a conveyance that had few springs was not so comfortable an undertaking as it is sometimes pictured. Furthermore you must not forget that it was also perilous, for not only was there danger from accident on these poorly constructed, unlighted thoroughfares but there was in addition the menace from highwaymen in the less populated districts. It took a great while to make a journey of any length, too, and to sleep in a coach where one was cramped, jolted, and either none too warm or miserably hot was not an unalloyed delight, as I am sure you will agree."

"I had not thought of any of those things," owned Stephen. "It just seemed on the face of it as if it must have been fun to ride on top of the coach and see the sights as one does from the Fifth Avenue or London buses."

"Oh," laughed his father, "a few hours' adventure like that is quite a different affair from making a stagecoach journey. I grant that to ride on a clear morning through the streets of a great city, or bowl along the velvet roads of a picturesque countryside as one frequently does in England is very delightful. To read Dickens' descriptions of journeys up to London is to long to don a greatcoat, wind a muffler about one's neck, and amid the cracking of whips and tooting of horns dash off behind the horses for the fairy city his pen portrays. Who would not have liked, for example, to set out with Mr. Pickwick for the Christmas holidays at Dingley Dell? Why, you cannot even read about it without seeing in your mind's eye the envious throng that crowded the inn yard and watched while the stableboys loosed the heads of the leaders and the steeds galloped away! And those marvelous country taverns he depicts, with their roaring fires, their steaming roasts, their big platters of fowl deluged in gravy, and their hot puddings! Was there ever writer more tantalizing?"

"You will have us all hungry in two minutes, Dad, if you keep on," exclaimed Stephen.

"And Dickens has us hungry, too," declared Mr. Tolman. "Nevertheless we must not forget that he paints but one side of the picture. He fails to emphasize what such a trip meant when the weather was cold and stormy, and those outside the coach as well as those inside it were often drenched with rain or snow, and well-nigh frozen to death. Moreover, while it is true that many of the inns along the turnpike were clean and furnished excellent fare, there were others that could boast nothing better than chilly rooms, damp beds, and only a very limited hospitality."

"I believe you are a realist, Henry," said his wife playfully.

Her husband laughed.

"Nor must we lose sight of the time consumed by making a trip by coach," he went on. "Business in those days was not such a rushing matter as it is now, of course; yet even when issues of importance were at stake, or crises of life and death were to be met, there was no hurrying things beyond a certain point. Physical impossibility prohibited it. Horses driven at their liveliest pace could cover only a comparatively small number of miles an hour; and at the points where the relays were changed, or the horses fed and rested; the mails deposited or taken aboard; and passengers left or picked up, there were unavoidable delays. In fact, the strongest argument against the stagecoach, and the one that influenced public opinion the most, was this so-called fast-mail service; for in order to make connections with other mail coaches along the route and not forfeit the money paid for doing so, horses were often driven at such a merciless rate of speed that the poor creatures became total wrecks within a very short time. Many a horse fell in its tracks in the inn yards, having been lashed along to make the necessary ten miles an hour and reach a specified town on schedule. Other horses were maimed for life. It is tragic to consider that in England before the advent of the railroad about thirty thousand horses were annually either killed outright or injured so badly that they were of little use afterward."

"Great Scott, Dad!" ejaculated Stephen.

"And England was no more guilty in this respect than was America, for in the early days of our own country when people were demanding quicker transportation and swifter mail service thousands of noble beasts offered up their last breath in making the required rate of speed."

"I suppose nobody thought about the horses," murmured the boy. "I am sure I didn't."

"If the public thought at all it was too selfish to care, I am afraid, until threatened by the possibility of the total extermination of these creatures," was his father's reply. "This danger, blended with a humane impulse which rose from the gentler-minded portion of the populace, was the decisive factor in urging men to seek out some other method of travel. Then, too, the world was waking up commercially and it was becoming imperative to find better ways for transporting the ever increasing supplies of merchandise. The quick moving of troops from one point to another was also an issue. Although the canals of England enabled the government to carry quite a large body of men, the method was a slow one. In 1806, for instance, it took exactly a week to shift troops from Liverpool to London, a distance of thirty-four miles."

"Why, they could have marched it in less time than that, couldn't they?" questioned Doris derisively.

"Yes, the journey might easily have been made on foot in two days," nodded her father. "But in war time a long march which exhausts the soldiers is frequently an unwise policy, for the men are in no condition when they arrive to go into immediate action, as reinforcements often must."

"I see," answered Doris.

"When the Liverpool and Manchester Railroad was opened in 1830 this thirty-four miles was covered in two hours," continued Mr. Tolman. "Of course the quick transportation of troops was then, as now, of very vital importance. We have had plenty of illustrations of that in our recent war against Germany. Frequently the fate of a battle has hung on large reinforcements being speedily dispatched to a weak point in the line. Moreover, by means of the railroads, vast quantities of food, ammunition and supplies of all sorts can constantly be sent forward to the men in action. During the late war our American engineers laid miles and miles of track under fire, thereby keeping open the route to the front so that there was no danger of the fighters being cut off and left unequipped. It was a service for which they, as well as our nation, won the highest praise. And not only was there a constant flow of supplies but it was by means of these railroads that hospital trains were enabled to carry to dressing stations far behind the lines thousands of wounded men whose lives might otherwise have been lost."

"I suppose the slightly wounded could be made more comfortable in this way, too," Mrs. Tolman suggested.

"Yes, indeed," was the reply. "Not only were the men better cared for in the roomier hospitals behind the lines, but as there was more space there the peril from contagion, always a menace when large numbers of sick are packed closely together, was greatly lessened; for there is nothing army doctors dread so much as an epidemic of disease when there is not enough room to isolate the patients."

"When did England adopt railroads in place of stagecoaches, Dad?" asked Doris presently.

At the question her father laughed.

"See here!" he protested good-humoredly, "what do you think I am? Just because I happen to be a superintendent do you think me a volume of railroad history, young woman? The topic, I confess, is a fascinating one; but I am off for a vacation to-day."

"Oh, tell us, Dad, do!" urged the girl.

"Nonsense! What is the use of spoiling a fine morning like this talking business?" objected her father.

"But it is not business to us," interrupted Mrs. Tolman. "It is simply a story—a sort of fairy tale."

"It is not unlike a fairy tale, that's a fact," reflected her husband gravely. "Imagine yourself back, then, in 1700, before steam power was in use in England. Now you must not suppose that steam had never been heard of, for an ancient Alexandrian record dated 120 **B.C.** describes a steam turbine, steam fountain, and steam boiler; nevertheless, Hero, the historian who tells us of them, leaves us in doubt as to whether these wonders were actually worked out, or if they were, whether they were anything but miniature models. Still the fact that they are mentioned goes to prove that there were persons in the world who at a very early date vaguely realized the possibilities of steam as a force, whether turned to practical uses or not. For years the subject remained an alluring one which led many a scientist into experiments without number. In various parts of the world men played with the idea and wrote about it; but no one actually produced any practical steam contrivance until 1650, when the second Marquis of Worcester constructed a steam fountain that could force the water from the moat around his castle as high as the top of one of the towers. The feat was looked upon as a marvel and afterward a larger fountain, similar in principle, was constructed at Vauxhall and from that time on the future of steam as a motive power was assured."

"Did the Marquis of Worcester go on with his experiments and make other things?" demanded Stephen.

"Apparently not," replied his father. "He did, nevertheless, furnish a basis for others to work on. Scientists were encouraged to investigate with redoubled zeal this strange vapor which, when controlled and directed, could carry water to the top of a castle tower. When in 1698 Savery turned Worcester's crude steam fountain to draining mines and carrying a water supply, every vestige of doubt that this mighty power could be applied to practical uses vanished."

"Did the steam engine come soon afterward?" queried Doris, who had become interested in the story.

"No, not immediately," answered Mr. Tolman, pausing to shift the gear of the car. "Before the steam engine, as we know it, saw the light, there had to be more experimenting and improving of the steam fountain. It was not until 1705 that Thomas Newcomen and his partner, John Calley, invented and patented the first real steam engine. Of course it was not in the least like the engines we use now. Still, it was a steam device with moving parts which would pump water, a tremendous advance over the mechanisms of the past where all the power had been secured by the alternate filling and emptying of a vacuum, or vacant receptacle, attached to the pump. Now, with Newcomen's engine a complete revolution took place. The engine with moving parts, the ancestor of our modern exquisitely constructed machinery, speedily crowded out the primitive steam fountain idea. The new device was very imperfect, there can be no question about that; but just as the steam fountain furnished the inspiration for the engine with moving parts, so this forward step became the working hypothesis for the engines that followed."

"What engines did follow?" Doris persisted, "and who did invent our steam engine?"

"Silly! And you in college," jeered Steve disdainfully.

"I am not taking a course in steam engines there," laughed his sister teasingly. "Anyway, girls are not expected to know who invented all the machines in the world, are they, Dad?"

Mr. Tolman waited a moment, then said soothingly:

"No, dear. Girls are not usually so much interested in scientific subjects as boys are—although why they should not be I never could quite understand. Nevertheless, I think it might be as well for even a girl to know to whom we are indebted for such a significant invention as the steam engine.

"It was James Watt," Stephen asserted triumphantly.

"It certainly was," his father agreed. "And since your brother has his information at his tongue's end, suppose we get him to tell us more about this remarkable person."

Stephen flushed.

"I'm afraid," began he lamely, "that I don't know much more. You see, I studied about him quite a long time ago and I don't remember the details. I should have to look it up. I do recall the name, though—"

His father looked amused.

"I don't know which of you children is the more blameworthy," remarked he in a bantering tone. "Doris, who never heard of Watt; or Stephen, who has forgotten all about him."

Both the boy and the girl chuckled good-humoredly.

"At least I knew his name, Dad—give me credit for that," piped Steve.

"That was something, certainly," Mrs. Tolman declared, joining in the laugh.

"Well, since neither of us can furnish the story, I don't see but that you will have to do it, Dad," Doris said mischievously.

"It would be a terrible humiliation if I should discover that I could not do it, wouldn't it?" replied Mr. Tolman with a smile. "In point of fact, there actually is not a great deal more that it is essential for one to know. It was by perfecting the engines of the Newcomen type and adding to them first one and then another valuable device that Watt finally built up the forerunner of our present-day engine. The progression was a gradual one. Now he would better one part, then some other. He surrounded the cylinder, for example, with a jacket, or chamber, which contained steam at the same pressure as that within the boiler, thereby keeping it as hot as the steam that entered it—a very important improvement over the old idea; then he worked out a plan by which the steam could be admitted at each end of the cylinder instead of at one end, as was the case with former engines. The latter innovation resulted in the push and pull of the piston rod. So it went."

"How did Watt come to know so much about engines?" asked Stephen.

"Oh, Watt was an engineer by trade—or rather he was a maker of mathematical instruments for the University of Glasgow, where he came into touch with a Newcomen engine. He also made surveys of rivers, harbors, and canals. So you see it was quite a consistent thing that a man with such a bent of mind should take up the pastime of experimenting with a toy like the steam engine in his leisure hours."

"Did he go so far as to patent it, Henry?" Mrs. Tolman questioned.

"Yes, he did. Many of our scientists either had not the wit to do this, alas, or else they were too impractical to appreciate the value of their ideas. In consequence the glory and financial benefit of what they did was often filched from them. But Watt was a Scotchman and canny enough to realize to some extent what his invention was worth. He therefore obtained a patent on it which was good for twenty-five years; and when, in 1800, this right expired he retired from business with both fame and fortune."

"It is nice to hear of one inventor who got something out of his toil," Mrs. Tolman observed.

"Indeed it is. Think of the many men who have slaved day and night, forfeited health, friends, and money to give to the world an idea, and never lived to receive either gratitude or financial reward, dying unknown or entirely forgotten. There is something tragic about the injustice of it. But Watt, I am glad to say, lived long enough to witness the service he had done mankind and enjoy an honored place among the great of the world."

"Is the kind of engine Watt invented now in use?" Doris inquired.

"Yes, that is a double-acting or reciprocating engine of a more perfect type," her father returned. "Mechanics and engineers went on improving Watt's engine just as he had improved those that had preceded it. It is interesting, too, to notice that after thousands of years scientists have again worked around to the steam turbine described so long ago in the Alexandrian records. This engine, although it does away with many of the moving parts introduced by Newcomen, preserves the essential principles of that early engine combined with Watt's later improvements. To-day we have a number of different kinds of engines, their variety differing with the purpose to which they are applied. Their cost, weight, and the space they require have been reduced and their power increased, and in addition we have made it possible to run them not only by means of coal or wood but by gasoline, oil, or electricity. We have small, light-weight engines for navigation use; mighty engines to propel our great warships and ocean liners; stationary engines for mills and power plants; to say nothing of the wonderful locomotive engines that can draw the heaviest trains over the highest of mountains. The principle of all these engines is, however, the same and for the brain behind them we must thank James Watt."

"Was it Watt who invented the locomotive, too?" ventured Doris. Her father shook his head.

"The perfecting of the locomotive, my dear, is, as Kipling says, another story."

"Tell it to us."

"Not now, daughter," protested Mr. Tolman. "I am far too hungry; and more than that I am eager to enjoy this beautiful country and forget railroads and locomotives."

"Did you say you were hungry, Henry?" asked Mrs. Tolman.

"I am—starved!" her husband said apologetically. "Isn't it absurd to be hungry so early in the day?"

"It is nearly noon, Dad!" said Steve, glancing down at the clock in the front of the car.

"Noon! Why, I thought it was still the middle of the morning."

"No, indeed! While you have been talking we have come many a mile, and the time has slipped past," his wife said. "If all goes well—" The shot from a bursting tire rent the air.

"Which evidently it does not," interrupted Mr. Tolman grimly, bringing the car to a stop. "How aggravating! We were almost into Palmer, where I had planned for us to lunch. Now it may be some little time before we can get anything to eat."

"Motorist's luck! Motorist's luck, my dear!" cried Mrs. Tolman gaily. "An automobilist must resign himself to taking cheerfully what comes."

"That is all very well," grumbled her husband, as he clambered out of the car. "Nevertheless you must admit that this mishap on the heels of the other one is annoying."

Stephen also got out and the two bent to examine the punctured tire.

"I should not mind so much if I were not so hungry," murmured Mr. Tolman. "How are you, Steve? Fainting away?"

The boy laughed.

"Well, I could eat something if I had it," he confessed.

"I wish I hadn't mentioned food," went on Mr. Tolman humorously. "It was an unfortunate suggestion."

"I'm hungry, too," piped Doris.

"There, you see the epidemic you have started, Henry," called Mrs. Tolman accusingly. "Here is Doris vowing she is in the last throes of starvation."

Nobody noticed that in the meanwhile the mother had reached down and lifted into her lap the small suitcase hidden in the bottom of the car. She opened the cover and began to remove its contents.

At length, when a remark her husband made to her went unheeded, he sensed her preoccupation and came around to the side of the car where she was sitting. Immediately he gave a cry of surprise.

"My word!" he exclaimed. "Steve, come here and see what your mother has."

Stephen looked.

There sat Mrs. Tolman, unpacking with quiet enjoyment sandwiches, eggs, cake, cookies, and olives.

A shout of pleasure rose from the famished travelers.

"So it was not your jewels, after all, Mater!" cried Stephen.

"No, and after the way you have slandered me and my little suitcase, none of you deserve a thing to eat," his mother replied. "However, I am going to be magnanimous if only to shame you. Now climb in and we will have our lunch. You can fix the tire afterward."

The men were only too willing to obey.

As with brightened faces they took their seats in the car, Stephen smiled with affection at his mother.

"Well, Mater, Watt was not the only person who lived to see himself appreciated; and I don't believe people were any more grateful to him for his steam engine than we are to you right now for this luncheon. You are the best mother I ever had."

CHAPTER IV

THE STORY OF THE FIRST RAILROAD

The new tire went on with unexpected ease and early afternoon saw the Tolmans once more bowling along the highway toward Northampton. The valley of the Connecticut was decked with harvest products as for an autumnal pageant. Stacks of corn dotted the fields and pyramids of golden pumpkins and scarlet apples made gay the verandas of the old homesteads or brightened the doorways of the great red barns flanking them.

"All that is needed to transform the scene into a giant Hallowe'en festival is to have a witch whisk by on a broomstick, or a ghost bob up from behind a tombstone," declared Mrs. Tolman. "Just think! If we had come by train we would have missed all this beauty."

"I see plainly that you do not appreciate the railroads, my dear," returned her husband mischievously. "This is the second time to-day that you have slandered them. You sound like the early American traveler who asserted that it was ridiculous to build railroads which did very uncomfortably in two days what could be done delightfully by coach in eight or ten."

"Why, I should have thought people who had never heard of motor-cars would have welcomed the quicker transportation the railroads offered," was Mrs. Tolman's reply.

"One would have thought so," answered Mr. Tolman. "Still, when we recall how primitive the first railroads were, the prejudice against them is not to be wondered at."

"How did they differ from those we have now, Dad?" Doris asked.

"In almost every way," answered her father, with a smile. "You see at the time Stephenson invented his steam locomotive nothing was known of this novel method of travel. As I told you, persons were accustomed to make journeys either by coach or canal. Then the steam engine was invented and immediately the notion that this power might be applied to transportation took possession of the minds of people in different parts of England. As a result, first one and then another made a crude locomotive and tried it out without scruple on the public highway, where it not only frightened horses but terrified the passers-by. Many an amusing story is told of the adventures of these amateur locomotives. A machinist named Murdock, who was one of James Watt's assistants, built a sort of grasshopper engine with very long piston rods and with legs at the back to help push it along; with this odd contrivance he ventured out into the road one night just at twilight. Unfortunately, however, his restless toy started off before he was ready to have it, and turning down an unfrequented lane encountered a timid clergyman who was taking a peaceful stroll and frightened the old gentleman almost out of his wits. The poor man had never seen a locomotive before and when the steaming object with its glowing furnace and its host of moving arms and legs came puffing toward him through the dusk he was overwhelmed with terror and screamed loudly for help."

A laugh arose from the listeners.

"And that is but one of the many droll experiences of the

first locomotive makers," continued Mr. Tolman. "For example Trevithick, another pioneer in the field, also built a small steam locomotive which he took out on the road for a trial trip. It chanced that during the experimental journey he and his fireman came to a tollgate and puffing up to the keeper with the baby steam engine, they asked what the fee would be for it to pass. Now the gate keeper, like the minister, had had no acquaintance with locomotives, and on seeing the panting red object looming like a specter out of the darkness and hearing a man's voice intermingled with its gasps and snorts, he shouted with chattering teeth:

"There is nothing to pay, my dear Mr. Devil! Just d-r-i-v-e along as f-a-s-t—as—ever—you—can."

His hearers applauded the story.

"Who did finally invent the railroad?" inquired Doris after the merriment had subsided.

"George Stephenson, an Englishman," replied her father. "For some time he had been experimenting with steam locomotives at the Newcastle coal mines where some agency stronger than mules or horses was needed to carry the products from one place to another. He had no idea of transporting people when he began to work out the suggestion. All he thought of was a coal train which would run on short lengths of track from mine to mine. But the notion assumed unexpected proportions until the Darlington road, the most ambitious of his projects, reached the astonishing distance of thirty-seven miles. When the rails for it were laid the engineer intended it should be used merely for coal transportation, as its predecessors had been; but some of the miners who lived along the route and were daily obliged to go back and forth to work begged that some sort of a conveyance be made that could also run along the track and enable them to ride to work instead of walking. So a little log house not unlike a log cabin, with a table in the middle and some chairs around it, was mounted on a cart that fitted the rails, and a horse was harnessed to the unique vehicle."

"And it was this log cabin on wheels that gave Stephenson his inspiration for a railroad train!" gasped Doris.

"Yes," nodded her father. "When the engineer saw the crude object the first question that came to him was why could not a steam locomotive propel cars filled with people as well as cars filled with coal. Accordingly he set to work and had several coach bodies mounted on trucks, installing a lever brake at the front of each one beside the coachman's box. In front of the grotesque procession he placed a steam locomotive and when he had fastened the coaches together he had the first passenger train ever seen."

"It must have been a funny looking thing!" Steve exclaimed, smiling with amusement at the picture the words suggested.

"It certainly was," agreed his father. "If you really wish to know how funny, some time look up the prints of this great-great-grandfather of our present-day Pullman and you will be well repaid for your trouble; the contrast is laughable."

"But was this absurd venture a success?" queried Mrs. Tolman incredulously.

"Indeed it was!" returned her husband. "In fact, Stephenson, like Watt, was one of the few world benefactors whose gift to humanity was instantly hailed with appreciation. The railroad was, to be sure, a wretched little affair when viewed from our modern standpoint, for there were no gates at the crossings, no signals, springless cars, and every imaginable discomfort. Fortunately, however, our ancestors had not grown up amid the luxuries of this era, and being of rugged stock that was well accustomed to hardships of every variety they pronounced the invention a marvel, which in truth it was.

"You've said it!" chuckled Steve in the slang of the day.

"In the meantime," went on Mr. Tolman, "conditions all over England were becoming more and more congested, and from every direction a clamor arose for a remedy. You see the invention of steam spinning machinery had greatly increased the output of the Manchester cotton mills until there was no such thing as getting such a vast bulk of merchandise to those who were eager to have it. Bales of goods waiting to be transported to Liverpool not only overflowed the warehouses but were even stacked in the open streets where they were at the mercy of robbers and storms. The canals had all the business they could handle, and as is always the result in such cases their owners became arrogant under their prosperity and raised their prices, making not the slightest attempt to help the public out of its dilemma. Undoubtedly something had to be done and in desperation a committee from Parliament sent for Stephenson that they might discuss with him the feasibility of building a railroad from Manchester to Liverpool. The committee had no great faith in the enterprise. Most of its members did not believe that a railroad of any sort was practical or that it could ever attain speed enough to be of service. However, it was a possibility, and as they did not know which way to turn to quiet the exasperated populace they felt they might as well investigate this remedy. It could do no harm."

Mr. Tolman paused as he stooped to change the gear of the car.

"So Stephenson came before the board, and one question after another was hurled at him. When, however, he was asked, half in ridicule, whether or not his locomotive could make thirty miles an hour and he answered in the affirmative, a shout of derision arose from the Parliament members. Nobody believed such a miracle possible. Nevertheless, in spite of their sceptical attitude, it was finally decided to build the Liverpool-Manchester road and about a year before its opening a date was set for a contest of locomotives to compete for the five-hundred-pound prize offered by the directors of the road."

"I suppose ever so many engines entered the lists," ventured Steve with interest.

"There were four," returned his father.

"And Stephenson drove one of them?"

"Yes."

"Oh, I hope it got the prize!" put in Doris eagerly.

Her father smiled at her earnestness.

"It did," was his reply. "Stephenson's engine was called the 'Rocket' and was a great improvement over the locomotive he had used at the mines, for this one had not only a steam blast but a multi-tubular boiler, a tremendous advance in engine building."

"I suppose that the winner of the prize not only got the money the road offered but his engine was the one chosen as a pattern for those to be used on the new railroad," ventured Stephen.

"Precisely. So you see a great deal depended on the showing each locomotive made. Unluckily in the excitement a tinder box had been forgotten, and when it came time to start, the spark to light the fires had to be obtained from a reading glass borrowed from one of the spectators. This, of course, caused some delay. But once the fires were blazing and steam up, the engines puffed away to the delight of those looking on."

"I am glad Stephenson was the winner," put in Doris.

"Yes," agreed her father. "He had worked hard and deserved success. It would not have seemed fair for some one else to have stolen the fruit of his toil and brain. Yet notwithstanding this, his path to fame was not entirely smooth. Few persons win out without surmounting obstacles and Stephenson certainly had his share. Not only was he forced to fight continual opposition, but the opening of the Manchester and Liverpool road, which one might naturally have supposed would be a day of great triumph, was, in spite of its success, attended by a series of catastrophes. It was on September 15, 1830, that the ceremonies took place, and long before the hour set for the gaily decorated trains to pass, the route was lined with excited spectators. The cities of Liverpool and Manchester also were thronged with those eager to see the engines start or reach their destination. There were, however, mingled with the crowd many persons who were opposed to the new venture."

"Opposed to it?" Steve repeated with surprise.

"Yes. It seems odd, doesn't it?"

"But why didn't they want a railroad?" persisted the boy. "I thought that was the very thing they were all demanding."

"You must not forget the condition of affairs at the time," said his father. "Remember the advent of steam machinery had deprived many of the cotton spinners of their jobs and in consequence they felt bitterly toward all steam inventions. Then in addition there were the stagecoach drivers who foresaw that if the railroads supplanted coaches they would no longer be needed. Moreover innkeepers were afraid that a termination of stage travel would lessen their trade."

"Each man had his own axe to grind, eh?" smiled Steve.

"I'm afraid so," his father answered. "Human nature is very selfish, and then as now men who worked for the general welfare regardless of their own petty preferences were rare. To the side of the enemies of the infant invention flocked every one with a grievance. The gentry argued that the installation of locomotives would frighten the game out of the country and ruin the shooting. Other opposers contended that the smoke from the engines would not only kill the birds but in time kill the patrons of the railroads as well. Still others protested that the sparks from the funnels might set fire to the fields of grain or to the forests. A swarm of added opponents dwelt on the fact that the passengers would be made ill by the lurching of the trains; that the rapid inrush of air would prevent their breathing; and that every sort of people would be herded together without regard to class,—the latter a very terrible calamity in a land where democracy was unknown. Even such intelligent men as the poet Wordsworth and the famous writer Ruskin came out hotly against the innovation, seeing in it nothing but evil."

"Didn't the opening of the Manchester and Liverpool Railroad convince the kickers they were wrong?" asked Steve.

"Unfortunately not," was Mr. Tolman's reply. "You see several unlucky incidents marred the complete success of the occasion. As the trains trimmed with bunting and flowers started out the scene seemed gay enough. On one car was a band of music; on another the directors of the road; and on still another rode the Duke of Wellington, who at that time was Prime Minister of England and had come down from London with various other dignitaries to honor the enterprise. Church bells rang, cannon boomed, and horns and whistles raised a din of rejoicing. But everywhere among the throng moved a large group of unemployed laborers who had returned from the Napoleonic wars in a discontented frame of mind and resented the use of steam machinery. They were on edge for trouble and if there were none they were ready to make it. So strong was the resentment of this element against the government that it seemed tempting

Providence for the Prime Minister to venture into the manu-facturing district of Manchester. At first it was decided that he would better omit the trip altogether; but on second thought it seemed wiser for him not to add fuel to the flames by disappointing the mill workers. The audience was in too ugly a mood to be angered. Therefore Wellington bravely resolved to carry out the program and ride in one of the open cars."

"I hope nothing happened to him, Dad!" gasped Doris breathlessly.

"Nothing beyond a good many minor insults and indignities," responded her father. "He was, however, in constant peril, and to those who bore the responsibility of the function he was a source of unceasing anxiety. But in spite of the jeers of the mob, their crowding and pushing about his car, he kept a smiling face like the true gentleman he was. Some of the rougher element even went so far as to hurl missiles at him. You can imagine how worried his friends were for his safety and how the directors who had invited him fidgeted. And as if this worry were not enough, by and by a fine rain began to fall and those persons riding in the open coaches, as well as the decorations and the spectators, got well drenched. Then there were delays on the turnouts while one train passed another; and as a climax to these discouragements, Mr. Hickson, a member of Parliament from Liverpool, got in the path of an approaching engine, became confused and was run over; and although Stephenson himself carried him by train to Liverpool he died that evening."

"I should call the fête to introduce the steam engine into England a most disastrous and forlorn one," remarked Mrs. Tolman.

"Well, in reality it was not such a failure as it sounds," replied her husband, "for only those most closely connected with it sensed the misfortunes that attended it. The greater part of the people along the route were good-humored and pleased; they marveled at the trains as they passed, cheered the Duke and the authorities with him, listened with delight to the band, and made a jest of the rain. A holiday crowd, you know, is usually quite patient. Hence the delays that fretted the guests and the officials of the road did not annoy the multitudes so vitally."

"Poor Stephenson really got some satisfaction out of the day then," sighed Mrs. Tolman.

"Oh, yes, indeed," said her husband. "Although I fancy the death of Mr. Hickson must have overshadowed his rejoicings. Notwithstanding this, however, the railroad proved itself a practical venture, which was the main thing. Such slight obstacles as the terror of the horses and the fact that the tunnels into Liverpool were so low that the engines had to be detached and the trains hauled into the yards by mules could be remedied."

A flicker of humor danced in Mr. Tolman's eyes.

"And did England begin to build railroads right away?" Steve inquired.

"Yes, and not only England but France also. Frenchmen who crossed the Channel took home glowing accounts of the novel invention and immediately the French Government realized that that country must also have railroads. But just as the conservative element in England had been sceptical and blocked Stephenson's progress—or tried to—so a corresponding faction in France did all it could to cry down the enterprise. Even those who upheld the introduction of the roads advocated them for only short distances out of Paris; a long trunk route they labeled as an absurdity. Iron was too expensive, they argued; furthermore the mountains of the country rendered extensive railroading impossible. France did not need railroads anyway.

Nevertheless the little group of seers who favored the invention persisted and there was no stopping the march of which they were the heralds. Railroads had come to stay and they stayed."

"It was a fortunate thing they did, wasn't it?" murmured Doris.

"A very fortunate thing," returned Mr. Tolman heartily. "Every great invention is usually suggested by a great need and so it was with this one. By 1836 the craze for railroad building swept both hemispheres. In England the construction of lines to most out-of-the-way and undesirable places were proposed, and the wildest schemes for propelling trains suggested; some visionaries even tried sails as a medium of locomotion instead of steam. Rich and poor rushed to invest their savings in railroads and alas, in many cases the misguided enthusiasts lost every shilling of their money in the project. Great business firms failed, banking houses were ruined, and thousands of workmen were thrown out of employment. In consequence a reaction followed and it was years before wary investors could again be induced to finance a railroad. In the interim both engines and coaches underwent improvement, especially the third-class carriage which in the early days was nothing more than an open freight car and exposed its unhappy patrons to snow, rain, and freezing weather."

"Great Scott!" cried Steve. "I should say there was room for improvement if that was the case."

"There was indeed," echoed his father. "In fact, it was a long time before travel by train became a pleasure. Most of the engines used pitch pine or soft coal as a fuel and as there were no guards on the smokestacks to prevent it, the smoke, soot, and cinders used to blow back from the funnels and shower the passengers. On the first railroad trip from New York to Albany those sitting outside the coaches were compelled to put up umbrellas to protect themselves from these annoyances."

"Imagine it!" burst out Doris, with a rippling laugh.

"Nor were the umbrellas of any service for long," continued Mr. Tolman, "for the sparks soon burned their coverings until nothing but the steel ribs remained."

"I don't wonder the trip was not a pleasure," smiled Mrs. Tolman.

"Yet, in spite of its discomfort, it was a novelty and you must not forget that, as I said before, the public of that period was a simple and less exacting one than is the public of to-day. We make a frightful fuss if we are jolted, chilled, crowded, delayed, or made uncomfortable; but our forefathers were a hale and hearty lot—less overworked perhaps, less nervous certainly, less indulged. They had never known anything better than cold houses, draughty and crowded stagecoaches, and stony highways—plenty of obstacles, you see, and few luxuries. Therefore with naïve delight they welcomed one new invention after another, overlooking its defects and considering themselves greatly blessed to have anything as fine. Probably we, who are a thousand per cent better off than they, do more grumbling over the tiny flaws in the mechanism of our lives than they did over the mammoth ones."

"Oh, come, Dad!" protested Stephen. "Aren't you putting it rather strong?"

"Not a whit too strong, Steve," Mrs. Tolman interrupted. "I believe we are a fussy, pampered, ungrateful generation. It is rather pathetic, too, to think it is we who now reap the benefits of all those perfected ideas which our ancestors enjoyed only in their most primitive beginnings. It seems hardly fair that Stephenson, for example, should never have seen a modern Pullman.

"He was spared something, wasn't he, Dad?" chuckled Steve mischievously.

But Mr. Tolman did not heed the remark.

"He had the vision," returned he softly, "the joy of seeing the marvel for the first time, imperfect as it was. Perhaps that was compensation enough. It is the reward of every inventor. Remember it is no mean privilege to stand upon the peak in Darien which Keats pictures."

CHAPTER V

STEVE LEARNS A SAD LESSON

No more disasters attended the journey and the travelers spun swiftly on to Northampton, arriving at the old New England town late in the afternoon. What a scene of activity the college campus presented! Bevies of girls, hatless and in gay-colored sweaters, drifted hither and thither, their laughter floating through the twilight with musical clearness. Occasionally some newcomer would join a group and a shout of welcome would hail her advent. Although Steve turned away from these gushing greetings with masculine scorn nevertheless he was far more interested in the novel picture than he would have been willing to admit. More than once he caught his eyes following a slender figure in white, across whose hair the sunset slanted, turning its blowing masses to a glory of gold. With what ease and freedom the girl moved! And when, as she passed, some one unceremoniously tossed her a ball and she caught it with swift accuracy, his admiration was completely won.

Steve speculated as to whether she would prove to be as pretty at close range as she was at a distance and decided not. Distance always brings a glamor with it. However, pretty or not, there was no disputing that she was a great favorite for every circle of students opened its magic ring at her approach and greeted her with a noisy clamor of affection. That she held herself with quiet reserve and was less demonstrative than those about her did not appear to lessen in the least their regard for her, and as Stephen watched he registered the wager that she was a person of more common sense than most girls.

Until recently it had been his habit to condemn the entire sex; but of late he had discovered that exceptions might be made to his rule. There were girls in the world worth noticing, even some worth talking to; and he felt certain that this attractive creature in white was one of them. However, it was an absurdity to be thinking about her now and quite beneath his dignity. But he meant sometime, when he could do so in casual fashion, to find out from Doris who she was. He had a curiosity to know what this person who looked as if she could row a boat, swim, and play tennis well, was called. Doris was always raving about her roommate, Jane Harden. She had said so much about her that he fairly detested the sound of her name. Now if only Jane Harden were a girl like this one, there would be some reason and excuse for being enthusiastic over her. To have this guest brought home to spend the Christmas holidays would be a pleasure to look forward to. How well she would skate and how gracefully; and how pretty she would be, especially if she had her hat off as she had now!

It was Doris who interrupted his reverie with the words:

"I hate to have you dear people go but I suppose you will have to. But do just wait long enough for me to see if I can't find Jane somewhere. She is crazy to meet my family and will scold me to death if I let you get away."

"I am afraid we can't stay but a moment or two, dear," objected Mrs. Tolman. "It is growing late, you know, and we must get to the hotel before it is too dark."

Bending forward she patted the boy's shoulder affectionately.

For an instant it seemed to Stephen as if every one in both cars must have heard the *pound, pound, pound* of his heart, as if everybody from Coventry to Torrington must have heard it. Helplessly he stared at Bud and Bud stared back. No words were needed to assure the two that once again they were linked together by misdoing as they often had been in the past. Bud looked anxiously toward his chum. He was a mischievous, happy-go-lucky lad but in his homely, freckled face there was a winsome manliness. Whatever the scrapes he got into through sheer love of fun it was characteristic of him that he was always courageous enough to confess to them. This was the first inkling he had had that Stephen had not acquainted his father with the escapade of the previous week and such a course was so at variance with his own frank nature that he was aghast. Even now he waited, expecting his pal would offer the true explanation of the mystery under discussion. He was ready to bear his share of the blame,—bear more than belonged to him if he could lighten Steve's sentence of punishment.

But the silence remained unbroken and the words he expected to hear did not come. A wave of surprise swept over his face, surprise followed by a growing scorn. It came to him in a flash that Stephen Tolman, the boy he had looked up to as a sort of idol, was a coward, a coward! He was afraid! It seemed impossible. Why, Steve was always in the thick of the football skirmishes, never shrinking from the roughness of the game; he was a fearless hockey player, a dauntless fighter. Coward was the last name one would have thought of applying to him. And yet here he sat cowering before the just result of his conduct. Bud was disappointed, ashamed; he turned away his head but not before the wretched lad who confronted him had caught in his glance the same contemptuous expression he had seen in O'Malley's face.

Again Stephen was despised and knew it.

Nevertheless it would not do to betray his secret now. He must not show that he was disconcerted. At every cost he must brazen out the affair. He had gone too far to do otherwise. He wondered as he sat there if any one suspected him; if his father, whose eye was as keen as that of an eagle, had put together any of the threads of evidence. He might be cherishing suspicions this very moment. It seemed impossible that he shouldn't. If only he would speak and have it over! Anything would be better than this suspense and uncertainty.

Mr. Tolman, however, maintained unwonted stillness and save for a restless twitching of his fingers on the wheel of the car did not move. If, thought Steve miserably, he could summon the nerve to look up, he would know in a second from his father's face whether he was annoyed or angry. At last the situation became unbearable and come what might he raised his eyes. To his amazement his father was sitting there quite serenely and so was everybody else, and the pause that seemed to him to stretch into hours had glided off as harmlessly and as naturally as other pauses. Apparently nobody was thinking about him, at least nobody but Bud. With a sigh of relief his tense muscles relaxed. He could trust Bud not to betray him. Once again he was safe!

"But I won't delay you a second, Mother—truly, I won't. I do want you to meet Jane. I'll ask the girls if they have seen her anywhere."

"If you get out into that mob they'll fall all over you and you'll never get back," growled Steve, who was beginning to feel hungry and was none too graciously inclined toward the prospective stranger.

"Oh, yes, I will," laughed Doris as she darted away.

In spite of this sanguine prediction, however, she did not return as promptly as she had promised, and Mr. Tolman began to fidget uneasily.

"We really ought to be starting on," he said at last. "Where is that child?"

"I knew she'd stop to admire everybody's new hat and talk over the whole summer," grumbled Steve scornfully.

"You are thinking of your dinner, son," his mother put in playfully.

"You bet I am! I'm hungry as a bear."

A pause followed in which visions of a big beefsteak with crisply fried potatoes blotted out every other picture from Steve's mind.

"Perhaps we ought not to have waited," he heard his mother murmur. "But I had not the heart to disappoint Doris. She is so fond of Jane and has talked so much about her! I had no idea it would take her so long to—"

"Here she comes!" Mr. Tolman broke in.

Stephen glanced up. Yes, there was Doris hurrying across the grass and beside her, walking with the same free and buoyant swing, was the girl of the golden hair,—Jane Harden.

With the same reserve and yet without a shadow of self-consciousness she came forward and in acknowledgment of the hurried introductions extended her hand with a grave smile of welcome; but both smile and gesture carried with them a sincerity very appealing. When she greeted Steve he flushed at being addressed as *Mr. Tolman* and mentally rose six inches in his boots. Yes, she was decidedly pretty, far prettier than she had been in the distance even. In all his life he had never seen a more attractive girl.

"I hope, Jane, that you are coming home with Doris for a visit sometime when your own family can spare you," he heard his mother say. "We all should like to have you."

"And I should like to come," was the simple and direct answer.

"Do plan on it then. Come any time that you can arrange to. We should very much enjoy having you, shouldn't we, Stephen?"

Stephen, so suddenly appealed to, turned very red and answered "Yes" in a tone that seemed to come gruffly from way down inside his chest, and then to the sound of hasty farewells the car started and shot out into the village street and the campus with its rainbow-hued occupants was lost to sight.

"A charming girl, isn't she?" Mrs. Tolman said to her husband. "So natural and unaffected! Doris says that she is quite the idol of the college and bids fair to be class president. I wish Doris would bring her home for the holidays."

Inwardly Steve echoed the sentiment but outwardly he preserved silence. He was too human a boy to dwell long on thoughts of any girl and soon Jane Harden was quite forgotten in the satisfaction of a steaming dinner and a comfortable bed, and the fairy journey of the next day when amid a splendor of crimson and gold the glories of Jacob's Ladder and the Mohawk Trail stretched before his eyes.

Within the week the big red car headed for Coventry and without a mishap rolled into the familiar main street of the town which never had seemed dearer than after the interval of absence. As the automobile sped past, friendly faces nodded from the sidewalks and hands were waved in greeting. Presently his mother called from the tonneau:

"Isn't that the Taylors' car, Henry, coming toward us? If it is do stop, for I want to speak to them."

Mr. Tolman nodded and slowed down the engine, at the same time putting out his hand to bring the on-coming car to a standstill. Yes, there were the Taylors, and on the front seat beside the chauffeur sat "Bud," the friend who had been most influential in coaxing Stephen into the dilemma of the past fortnight. It was Bud, Steve could not forget, who had been the first to drop out of the car when trouble had befallen and who had led the other boys off on foot with him to Torrington. The memory of his chum's treacherous conduct still rankled in Steve's mind. He had not spoken to him since. But now here the two boys were face to face and unless they were to betray to their parents that something was wrong they must meet with at least a semblance of cordiality. The question was which of them should be the first to make the advance.

Twice Bud cleared his throat and appeared to be on the verge of uttering a greeting when he encountered Stephen's scowl and lost courage to call the customary: "Ah, there, Stevie!"

And Stephen, feeling that right was on his side and being too proud to open the conversation, could not bring himself to say: "Hi, Bud!" as he always did.

As a result the schoolmates simply glared at each other.

Fortunately their elders were too much occupied with friendly gossip to notice them and it was not until the talk shifted abruptly into a channel that appalled both boys that their glance met with the sympathy of common danger.

It was Bud's mother from whose lips the terrifying words innocently fell.

"Havens ill and you in New York Wednesday!" she exclaimed incredulously. "But I certainly thought I saw your car turning into the gate that very afternoon."

"I guess not, my dear," asserted Mrs. Tolman tranquilly. "The car has not been out of the garage until now. It must have been somebody else you saw."

"But it was your car—I am certain of it," persisted Mrs. Taylor.

"Nonsense, Mary!" laughed her husband. "If the car has been in the garage for a week how could it have been. You probably dreamed it. You want a big red car so much yourself that you see them in your sleep."

"No, I don't," protested Mrs. Taylor smiling good-humoredly at her husband's banter.

"Well, it may have been the Woodworths'," Mrs. Tolman said with soothing inspiration. "They have a car like ours and Mrs. Woodworth came to call while I was away. I'll ask the maid when I get home."

"Y-e-s, it may have been the Woodworths'," admitted Mrs. Taylor reluctantly. It was plain, however, that she was unconvinced. "But I could have staked my oath that it was your car and Steve driving it," she added carelessly.

"Steve!" Mr. Tolman ejaculated.

"Oh, Steve never drives the car," put in Mrs. Tolman quickly. "He is not old enough to have a license yet, you know. That proves absolutely that you were mistaken. But Stephen has run the car now and then when Havens or his father were with him and he does very well at it. Some day he will be driving it alone, won't you, son?"

Bending forward she patted the boy's shoulder affectionately.

For an instant it seemed to Stephen as if every one in both cars must have heard the *pound, pound, pound* of his heart, as if everybody from Coventry to Torrington must have heard it. Helplessly he stared at Bud and Bud stared back. No words were needed to assure the two that once again they were linked together by misdoing as they often had been in the past. Bud looked anxiously toward his chum. He was a mischievous, happy-go-lucky lad but in his homely, freckled face there was a winsome manliness. Whatever the scrapes he got into through sheer love of fun it was characteristic of him that he was always courageous enough to confess to them. This was the first inkling he had had that Stephen had not acquainted his father with the escapade of the previous week and such a course was so at variance with his own frank nature that he was aghast. Even now he waited, expecting his pal would offer the true explanation of the mystery under discussion. He was ready to bear his share of the blame,—bear more than belonged to him if he could lighten Steve's sentence of punishment.

But the silence remained unbroken and the words he expected to hear did not come. A wave of surprise swept over his face, surprise followed by a growing scorn. It came to him in a flash that Stephen Tolman, the boy he had looked up to as a sort of idol, was a coward, a coward! He was afraid! It seemed impossible. Why, Steve was always in the thick of the football skirmishes, never shrinking from the roughness of the game; he was a fearless hockey player, a dauntless fighter. Coward was the last name one would have thought of applying to him. And yet here he sat cowering before the just result of his conduct. Bud was disappointed, ashamed; he turned away his head but not before the wretched lad who confronted him had caught in his glance the same contemptuous expression he had seen in O'Malley's face.

Again Stephen was despised and knew it.

Nevertheless it would not do to betray his secret now. He must not show that he was disconcerted. At every cost he must brazen out the affair. He had gone too far to do otherwise. He wondered as he sat there if any one suspected him; if his father, whose eye was as keen as that of an eagle, had put together any of the threads of evidence. He might be cherishing suspicions this very moment. It seemed impossible that he shouldn't. If only he would speak and have it over! Anything would be better than this suspense and uncertainty.

Mr. Tolman, however, maintained unwonted stillness and save for a restless twitching of his fingers on the wheel of the car did not move. If, thought Steve miserably, he could summon the nerve to look up, he would know in a second from his father's face whether he was annoyed or angry. At last the situation became unbearable and come what might he raised his eyes. To his amazement his father was sitting there quite serenely and so was everybody else, and the pause that seemed to him to stretch into hours had glided off as harmlessly and as naturally as other pauses. Apparently nobody was thinking about him, at least nobody but Bud. With a sigh of relief his tense muscles relaxed. He could trust Bud not to betray him. Once again he was safe!

CHAPTER VI

MR. TOLMAN'S SECOND YARN

For a day or two it seemed to Stephen that he would never cease to be haunted by the shame and regret that followed his confiscation of the big red touring car, or forget the good resolutions he made in consequence; but within an incredibly short time both considerations were thrust into the background by the rush of life's busy current. School and athletics kept him occupied so that he had little leisure for thought, and when he was in the house his father and mother smiled on him as affectionately as before, which did much to restore to him his normal poise. Long ago the boys had dropped the motor-car episode from their memories and even Bud Taylor did not refer to it when he and Steve came together to organize the hockey team for the approaching matches.

In the meantime the Thanksgiving holidays were drawing near and Mr. Tolman suggested that he and Stephen should run over to New York for a short visit. With the prospect of so much pleasure was it strange the boy ceased to dwell on the unhappiness of the past or the possibility of disaster in the future? The coming journey to New York was, to be sure, no great novelty, for Stephen had often accompanied his father there on business excursions; nevertheless such an outing was a treat to which he looked forward as a sort of Arabian Nights adventure when for a short time he stayed at a large hotel, ate whatever food pleased his fancy, and went sight-seeing and to innumerable "shows" with his father. He was wont to return to Coventry after the holiday with a throng of happy memories and many a tale of marvels with which to entertain the boys.

Therefore when he and his father boarded the express Thanksgiving week the lad was in the highest spirits.

"Motor-cars are all very well," observed Mr. Tolman, as the porter stowed their luggage away, "but on a cold night like this a Pullman car on a well-laid track is not to be despised. Eh, son?"

"I don't believe that I should want to travel to New York in a touring-car at this time of year," agreed Stephen, smiling.

"It is getting too late in the season to use an open car, anyway," rejoined his father. "I have delayed putting the car up because I have been hoping we might have a little more warm weather; but I guess the warm days have gone and the winter has come to stay now."

"But there is no snow yet, Dad."

"No. Still it is too chilly to drive with any comfort. The Taylors shipped their car off last week and when I get home I shall do the same."

Stephen looked disappointed.

"I don't mind the cold when I'm wrapped up," he ventured.

"You are not at the wheel, son," was his father's quick retort. "The man who is has his fingers nipped roundly, I can assure you. It is a pity we have become so soft and shrink so from discomfort. Think what our forbears endured when they went on journeys!"

"Neither the English stagecoaches nor Stephenson's railroad could have been very comfortable, to judge from your descriptions of them," laughed Steve.

"Oh, don't heap all the blame on the English," his father replied. "Our own modes of travel in the early days were quite as bad as were those on the other side of the water."

"I wish you would tell me about the first American railroads," said the boy. "I was wondering about them the other night."

Mr. Tolman settled back in his seat thoughtfully.

"America," he answered presently, "went through a pioneer period of railroading not unlike England's. Many strange steam inventions were tried in different parts of the country, and many fantastic scientific notions put before the public. Even previous to Watt's steam engine Oliver Evans had astonished the quiet old city of Philadelphia by driving through its peaceful streets in a queer steam vehicle, half carriage and half boat, which he had mounted on wheels. Evans was an ingenious fellow, a born inventor if ever there was one, who worked out quite a few steam devices, some of which Watt later improved and adopted. Then in 1812 John Stevens of New York got interested in the steam idea and urged the commissioners of his state to build a railroad between Lake Erie and Albany, suggesting that a steam engine not unlike the one that propelled the Hudson River ferryboats could be used as power for the trains. He was enthusiastic over the scheme but the New York officials had no faith in the proposition, insisting that a steam locomotive could never be produced that would grip the rails with sufficient tension to keep cars on the track or draw a heavy load."

"They'd better have given the plan a showdown," interrupted Steve grimly.

"No doubt that is true," admitted his father. "However, it is very easy for us, with our knowledge of science, to look back and laugh at their mistakes. The world was very new in those days and probably had we lived at that time and been equally ignorant of railroads and engines we should have been just as cautious and unbelieving. The railroad was still a young invention, you must remember, and to many persons it seemed a rather mad, uncertain enterprise."

"When was the first American railroad built?" inquired the lad.

"If by a railroad you mean something which moved along rails like a tram-car, the first such road was built at Quincy, Mass., in 1826; but it was not a steam railroad. It was merely a train of cars drawn by horses along a track that spanned a series of stone ties. Nor was it very extensive in length. In fact, it was only three miles long and probably would not have been built at all if the question had not arisen as to how the heavy blocks of granite necessary for the construction of Bunker Hill monument were to be carried from the quarries to the Neponset River, the point from which they were to be shipped to Charlestown. Bryant, the builder of the road, had heard of Stephenson's successful use of tracks at the Newcastle coal mines and saw no reason why a road of similar pattern could not be laid from the quarries to the ship landing. If such a plan could be worked out, he argued, it would be a great saving of time and labor. Accordingly the railroad was built at a cost of more than ten thousand dollars a mile and it unquestionably performed the service required of it even if it did necessitate the expenditure of a good deal of money. Since the grade sloped toward the river the heavily loaded cars moved down the tracks very easily and as they were empty on their return the ascent was made with equal ease. All the year round this quaint railroad was in constant use, a snowplow being attached to the front car in winter to clear the deep snow from the tracks."

"I suppose that was the first railroad snowplow, too," observed Stephen.

"I suppose it was," his father agreed. "For some time afterward this old road with its granite ties was the model from which American engineers took their inspiration, it being many years before railroad builders realized that wooden ties were more flexible and made a better, even though less durable roadbed."

"Were any more railroads like the Quincy road built in America?" questioned Steve.

"Yes, a railroad very much like it was built in the Pennsylvania mining country to transport coal from the mines at Summit down to the Lehigh Valley for shipment. An amusing story is told of this railroad, too. It extended down the mountainside in a series of sharp inclines between which lay long stretches of level ground. Now you know when you coast downhill your speed will give you sufficient impetus to carry you quite a way on a flat road before you come to a stop. So it was with this railroad. But the force the cars gained on the hillside could not carry them entirely across these long levels, and therefore platform cars were built on which a number of mules could be transported and later harnessed to the cars to pull them across the flat stretches. At the end of each level the mules would be taken aboard again and carried down to the next one, where they were once more harnessed to the cars. Now the tale goes that to the chagrin of the railroad people the mules soon grew to enjoy riding so much that they had no mind to get out and walk when the level places were reached and it became almost impossible to make them. All of which proves the theory I advanced before—that too much luxury is not good for any of us and will even spoil a perfectly good mule."

Steve chuckled in response.

"I'm afraid with railroads like these America did not make much progress," he said.

"No very rapid strides," owned his father. "Nevertheless men were constantly hammering away at the railroad idea. In out-of-the-way corners of the country were many persons who had faith that somehow, they knew not how, the railroad would in time become a practical agency of locomotion. When the Rainhill contest of engines took place in England before the opening of the Liverpool-Manchester road, and Stephenson carried off the prize, Horatio Allen, one of the engineers of the Delaware and Hudson Canal Company, was sent over to examine the locomotives competing and if possible buy one for a new railroad they hoped to put into operation. Unluckily none of the engines were for sale but he was able to purchase at Stourbridge a steam locomotive and this he shipped to New York. It reached there in 1829—a ridiculous little engine weighing only seven tons. Before its arrival a track of hemlock rails fastened to hemlock ties had been laid and as the Lackawanna River lay directly in the path of the proposed road a wooden trestle about a hundred feet high had been built across the river. This trestle was of very frail construction and calculated to sustain only a four-ton engine and therefore when the seven-ton locomotive from Stourbridge arrived and was found to weigh nearly double that specification there was great consternation."

"Did they tear the trestle down and build another?" asked Steve with much interest.

Mr. Tolman did not heed the question.

"Now in addition to the disconcerting size of the engine," he continued, "the wooden rails which had been laid during the previous season had warped with the snows and were in anything but desirable condition. So altogether the prospect of trying out the enterprise, on which a good deal of money had already been spent, was not only disheartening but perilous."

"The inspectors or somebody else would have put an end to such a crazy scheme jolly quick if it had been in our day, wouldn't they?" grinned the boy.

"Yes, nobody could get very far with anything so unsafe now," his father responded. "But all this happened before the era of inspectors, construction laws, or the *Safety First* slogan. Hence no one interfered with Horatio Allen. If he chose to break his neck and the necks of many others as well he was free to do so. Therefore, nothing daunted, he got up steam in his baby engine, which was the more absurd for having painted at its front a fierce red lion, and off he started—along his hemlock railroad. The frail bridge swayed and bent as the locomotive rumbled over it but by sheer miracle it did not give way and Allen reached the other side without being plunged to the bottom of the river."

Steve drew a long breath of relief.

"Did they go on using the railroad after that?" he asked.

His father shook his head.

"No," he replied. "Although every one agreed that the demonstration was a success the wooden rails were not durable enough to last long and the company was not rich enough to replace them with metal ones. Therefore, in spite of Allen's pleas and his wonderful exhibition of courage, the road fell into disuse, the engine was taken apart, and the enterprise abandoned."

"What a pity!"

"Yes, it was, for had New York persevered in this undertaking the railroad might have made its advent in the United States much sooner than it did. As it was, once again, like a meteor, the experiment flashed into sight and disappeared with success well within reach."

"And who was the next promoter?"

"Peter Cooper was the next experimenter of note," Mr.

Tolman answered, "and his adventure with railroading was entertaining, too. He lived in Baltimore and being of a commercial trend of mind he decided that if a railroad could be built through the Potomac Valley and across the Alleghany Mountains it might win back for his state the trade that was rapidly being snatched away by the Erie and Pennsylvania Canal. With this idea in mind Cooper built thirteen miles of track and after experimenting with a sort of tram-car and finding it a failure he had a car made that should be propelled by sails."

"Sails!" gasped Steve.

His father smiled at his astonishment.

"Yes, sails!" he repeated. "Into this strangely equipped vehicle he invited some of the editors of the Baltimore papers, and little sensing what was before them the party set forth on its excursion."

"Did the car go?"

"Oh, it went all right!" chuckled Mr. Tolman. "The trouble was not with its *going*. The difficulty was that as it flew along the rails a cow suddenly loomed in its pathway and as she did not move out of the way of the approaching car she and the railroad pioneers came into collision. With a crash the car toppled over and the editors, together with the enraged Peter Cooper, were thrown out into the mud. Of course the affair caused the public no end of laughter but to Cooper and his guests it proved convincingly that sails were not a desirable substitute for steam power."

"I suppose Cooper then went to work to build some other kind of a railroad," mused Steve.

"That is exactly what he did," was the rejoinder. "He did not, however, do this deliberately but rather fell into a dilemma that left him no other choice. You see a group of men coaxed him to buy some land through which it was expected the new Baltimore and Ohio Railroad was to pass. These prospectors figured that as the road was already started and a portion of the wooden track laid, the railroad was a sure thing, and by selling their land to the railroad authorities they would be enabled to turn quite a fortune for themselves. In all good faith Cooper had joined the company and then, after discovering that the railroad men had apparently abandoned their plan to build, in dastardly fashion, one after another of the promoters wriggled out of the enterprise and left poor Peter Cooper with a large part of his money tied up in a worthless, partially constructed railroad."

"What a rotten trick!" cried Steve.

"Yes; and yet perhaps Cooper deserved a little chastisement," smiled Mr. Tolman. "Instead of making money out of other people as he had intended—"

"He got stung himself!" burst out the boy.

"Practically so, yes," was the reply. "Well, at any rate, there he was and if he was ever to get back any of his fortune he must demonstrate that he had profound faith in the partly constructed railroad. Accordingly he bought a small engine weighing about a ton—"

"One ton!"

"So small that it was christened the 'Tom Thumb.' He now had his wooden rails and his pygmy engine but was confronted by still another perplexity. The railroad must pass a very abrupt curve, it was unavoidable that it should do so—a curve so dangerous that everybody who saw it predicted that to round it without the engine jumping the track and derailing the cars behind would be impossible. Poor Peter Cooper faced a very discouraging problem. There was no gainsaying that the curve was a bad one; moreover, his locomotive was not so perfect a product as he might have wished. It had been built under his direction and consisted of the wee engine he had bought in New York connected with an iron boiler about the size of an ordinary tin wash boiler; and as no iron piping was made in America at this time Cooper had taken some old steel musket barrels as a substitute for tubing. With this crude affair he was determined to convince the public that a steam railroad was a workable proposition."

"He had a nerve!"

"It took nerve to live and accomplish anything in those days," returned Mr. Tolman. "In the first place few persons had fortunes large enough to back big undertakings; and in addition America was still such a young country that it had not begun to produce the materials needed by inventors for furthering any very extensive projects. In fact the world of progress was, as Kipling says, 'very new and all.' Hence human ingenuity had to make what was at hand answer the required purpose, and as a result Peter Cooper's Tom Thumb engine, with its small iron boiler and its gun-barrel tubing, was set upon the wooden track, and an open car (a sort of box on wheels with seats in it) was fastened to it. Into this primitive conveyance the guests invited for the occasion clambered. Ahead lay the forbidding curve. Stephenson, the English engineer, had already stated mathematically the extreme figure at which a curve could be taken and the locomotive still remain on the track, and Peter Cooper was well aware that the curve he must make was a far worse one. However, it would never do for him to betray that he had any misgivings. Therefore, together with his guests, he set out on his eventful trip which was either to demolish them all, or convince the dignitaries of the railroad company that not only was a steam railroad practical but that the Baltimore and Ohio Road was a property valuable enough to be backed by capital."

Steve leaned forward, listening eagerly to the story.

"Slowly the little engine started, and nearer and nearer came the terrible curve. The train was now running at fifteen miles an hour, a speed almost unbelievable to the simple souls of that time. Round the curve it went in safety, increasing its velocity to eighteen miles an hour. The railroad officials who were Cooper's guests were frantic with enthusiasm. One man produced paper and pencil and begged those present to write their names, just to prove that it was possible to write even when flying along at such a meteoric rate of speed. Another man jotted down a few sentences to demonstrate that to think and write connected phrases were things that could be done, in spite of the fact that one was dashing through space with this unearthly rapidity."

"So the railroad men were converted, were they?"

"They were more than converted; they were exultant," said his father. "Of course it was some time after this before the Baltimore and Ohio Railroad became a reality. Capital had to be raised and the project stably launched."

"Oh, then this was not the first railroad in the country, after all," observed the boy in a disappointed tone.

"No. South Carolina boasts the first regular passenger locomotive propelled by steam," returned Mr. Tolman. "This road ran from Charleston to Hamburg and although a charter was obtained for it in 1827 it took all the first year to lay six miles of track. In fact it was not until 1830 that the railroad began to be operated to any extent. When it was, a locomotive, every part of which had been produced in this country, was employed to draw the trains. This was the first steam locomotive of American make in history. It was dubbed 'The Best Friend' and, like the engines that had preceded it, had a series of interesting adventures. Since it was the only locomotive in the possession of the road and was in use all day any repairs on the hard-worked object had to be made at night."

"Humph!" ejaculated Stephen.

"Nevertheless 'The Best Friend' might have gone on its way prosperously had it not been for the ignorance of those who ran it. The engineer, to be sure, understood more or less about a steam locomotive although he was none too wise; but the fireman, unfortunately, understood next to nothing, and one day, on being left alone in the cab and seeing the steam escaping from the safety valve, he conceived the notion that a leak was causing unnecessary waste. Therefore he securely screwed up the space through which the steam had been issuing, and to make prevention more certain he himself, a large and heavy man, sat down on the escape valve."

"And presto!" exclaimed Steve, rubbing his hands.

"Exactly so! Presto, indeed! Figuratively speaking, he blew sky-high and 'The Best Friend' with him," replied Mr. Tolman. "It was an unfortunate happening, too, for people were still ill-informed about the uses of steam and very nervous about its mysterious power and this accident only served to make them more so. For some time afterward many persons refused to patronize the railroad in spite of all the authorities could do to soothe them. In time, however, the public calmed down, although in order to reassure them it was found necessary to put a car heaped with bales of cotton between them and the engine, not only to conceal the monster from their view but also to convince them that it was some distance away. Whether they also had a vague notion that in case they went skyward the cotton might soften their fall when they came down, I do not know."

"Railroading certainly had its troubles, didn't it?" Steve commented with amusement.

"It certainly had, especially in our own country," was the reply. "In England Stephenson and other experimenters like him had materials at hand which to some extent served their purpose; moreover, thanks to Watt and other inventors, there were definite scientific ideas to work from. But in America the successful railroad which might serve as a model was unknown. Therefore for some time English engines continued to be shipped across the sea, and even then it was a long time before our American engineers understood much about their mechanism. Only by means of repeated experiments, first in one part of the country and then in another, did our American railroads, so marvelous in their construction, come into being."

Mr. Tolman paused a moment, yawned, and then rose and beckoned to the porter.

"We still have much to perfect in our modern railroad, however," he said with a touch of humor. "The sleeping car, for example, is an abomination, as you are speedily to have proved to you. Here, porter! We'd like these berths made up. I guess we'd better turn in now, son. You have had enough railroading for one day and are tired. You must get a rest and be in the pink of condition to-morrow for, remember, you are going to wake up in New York."

"If it will make to-morrow come any quicker I am quite ready to go to bed," retorted Stephen, with a sleepy smile.

CHAPTER VII

A HOLIDAY JOURNEY

The next morning, when Steve woke to the swaying of the train and a drowsy sense of confusion and smoke, he could not for an instant think where he was; but it did not take long for him to open his eyes, recollect the happenings of the previous day, smile with satisfaction, and hurriedly wriggle into his clothes.

Already he could hear his father stirring in the berth below and presently the elder man called:

"We shall be in New York in half-an-hour, son, so get your traps packed up. How did you sleep?"

"Sound as a top!"

"That is fine! I was afraid you might not rest very well. As I observed last night, a sleeping car is not all that it might be. The day will come when it will have to be improved. However, since it gets us to New York safely and economizes hours of day travel, it is a blessing for which we should be grateful."

As he spoke he moved into the aisle and helped the boy down from his perch; they then sought out a distant seat where they dropped down and watched the rapidly passing landscape.

"I have been thinking, as I was dressing, of the story you told me last night about our American railroads," said the lad. "It surprised me a good deal to hear that the South took the lead over the North in the introduction of the steam locomotive."

Mr. Tolman smiled into the eager face.

"While it is true that South Carolina took the initiative in railroading for a short time the South did not remain long in the ascendency," he answered, "for the third steam locomotive put into actual passenger service was built at Albany. This city, because of its geographical position, was a great stagecoach center, having lines that radiated from it into the interior in almost every direction. And not only was it an important coaching rendezvous but as it was also a leading commercial tributary of New York, the Mohawk and Hudson Railroad had built a short track between Albany and Schenectady and supplied it with cars propelled by horse power. Now in 1831 the company decided to transform this road into a steam railroad and to this end ordered a steam locomotive called the 'DeWitt Clinton' to be constructed at West Point with the aim of demonstrating to the northern States the advantages of steam transportation. You can imagine the excitement this announcement caused. Think, if you had never seen a steam engine, how eager you would be to behold the wonder. These olden time New Yorkers felt precisely the same way. Although the route was only sixteen miles long the innovation was such a novel and tremendous one that all along the way crowds of spectators assembled to watch the passing of the magic train. At the starting point near the Hudson there was a dense throng of curious onlookers who gathered to see for the first time in all their lives the steam locomotive and its brigade of coaches,—for in those days people never spoke of a train of cars; a group of railroad carriages was always known as a brigade, and the term *coach* was, and in many cases still is applied to the cars. This train that created so much interest was practically like Stephenson's English trains, being made up of a small locomotive, a tender, and two carriages constructed by fastening stagecoach bodies on top of railroad trucks. Stout iron chains held these vehicles together—a primitive, and as it subsequently proved, a very impractical method of coupling."

"It must have been a funny enough train!" Steve exclaimed.

"I doubt if it appeared so to the people of that time," his father returned, "for since the audience of that period had nothing with which to compare it, it probably seemed quite the ordinary thing. Was it not like the railroad trains used in England? How was America to know anything different? Yes, I am sure the 'DeWitt Clinton' was considered a very grand affair indeed, even though it was only a small engine without a cab, and had barely enough platform for the engineer to stand upon while he drove the engine and fed the pitch-pine logs into the furnace."

"How many people did the train hold?" inquired Steve, with growing curiosity.

"Each coach carried six persons inside and two outside," was Mr. Tolman's reply, "and on this first eventful trip not quite enough adventurous souls could be found to fill the seats. Perhaps could the unwary passengers who did go have foreseen the discomforts ahead of them there would have been fewer yet. But often ignorance is bliss. It certainly was so in this case for in high feather the fortunate ones took their places, the envied of many a beholder."

"What happened?" asked the boy eagerly. "Was the trip a success?"

"That depends on what you mean by success," laughed his father. "If you are asking whether the passengers arrived safely at Schenectady I can assure you that they did; but if you wish to know whether the journey was a comfortable one, and likely to convert the stranger to steam travel, that is quite another matter. The description of the excursion which history has handed down to us is very naïve. In the first place the pitch-pine fuel sent a smudge of smoke and cinders back over all the passengers and if it did not entirely choke them it at least encrusted them thickly with dirt, particularly the ones who sat outside. The umbrellas they opened to protect themselves were soon demolished, their coverings being blown away or burned up by the sparks. In fact, it was only by continual alertness that the clothing of the venturesome travelers was not ignited. In the meantime those inside the coaches fared little better, for as the coaches were without springs and the track was none too skilfully laid, the jolting of the cars all but sent the heads of the passengers through the roof of the coaches. Added to this the train proceeded in a series of jerks that wrenched the chains and banged one coach into another with such violence that those outside were in danger of being hurled down upon the track, and those inside were tossed hither and thither from seat to seat. You will easily comprehend that the outing was not one of unalloyed pleasure."

The boy laughed heartily.

"Of course," went on Mr. Tolman, "there was no help for anybody until the first stopping place was reached; but when the engine slowed down and the grimy, almost unrecognizable pilgrims had a chance to catch their breath, something had to be done by way of a remedy. The remedy fortunately was near at hand and consisted of nothing very difficult. Some of the more enterprising of the company leaped out and tore the rails from a near-by fence and after stretching the coupling chains taut, they bound them to the wooden boards. In this way the coaches were kept apart and the silk hats of the dignitaries who had been invited to participate in the opening of the road rescued from total annihilation."

"I'll bet everybody was glad to disembark at Schenectady," declared Stephen.

"I'll wager they were! They must have been exhausted from being jounced and jostled about. Nevertheless the novelty of the adventure probably brought its own compensations, and they were doubtless diverted from their woes by the sight of the cheering and envious spectators, the terrified horses, and the open-mouthed children that greeted them wherever they went."

"But the promoters could hardly expect the public to be very keen for a steam railroad after such an exhibition," reflected Steve.

"Fortunately our forefathers were not as critical as you," said his father, "and in consequence the coach line from Albany to Schenectady was speedily supplanted by a steam railroad, as were the various coach lines into the interior of the State. As a result hundreds of broken-down coach horses were turned out to pasture, a merciful thing. Gradually a series of short steam railway lines were constructed from one end of the State to the other, until in 1851 these were joined together to make a continuous route to Lake Erie. Perhaps we have only scant appreciation of the revolution that came with this advance in transportation. It meant the beginning of travel and commerce between the eastern States and those in the interior of the country; it also meant the speedy shipment of eastern products to the West, where they were greatly needed, and the reception of western commodities in the East. But more than all this, it signified a bond of fellowship between the scattered inhabitants of the same vast country who up to this time had been almost total strangers to one another, and was a mighty stride in the direction of national loyalty and sympathy. Therefore it was entirely seemly that Millard Fillmore, then President of the United States, and Daniel Webster, the Secretary of State, should be honored guests at the celebration that attended the opening of the railroad."

"Did the road reach no farther than Lake Erie?" asked Stephen.

"Not at first," replied his father. "From that point commerce was carried on by means of ships on the Great Lakes. But in time western railroad companies began to build short stretches of track which later on they joined together as the other railroad builders had done."

"Did the line go all the way across the country?"

"Oh, no, indeed. Our trans-continental railroads were a mighty project in themselves and their story is a romance which I will tell you some other time. Before such stupendous enterprises could be realities, our young, young country had a vast deal of growing to do, and its infant railroads and engineering methods had to be greatly improved. So long as we still built roads where the rails were liable to come up through the floor and injure the passengers, and where the tracks were not strongly enough constructed to resist floods and freshets, our steam locomotion could not expect any universal degree of popularity."

"I don't suppose, though, that the cows continued to tip the cars over and turn the passengers out into the dirt as they did in the days of Peter Cooper," mused Steve thoughtfully.

"They may not have derailed the trains," his father replied quite seriously, "but they often did delay them. Nor could the passengers be blamed for finding fault with the unheated cars, or the fact that sometimes, when it snowed hard, the engineer ran his engine under cover and refused to go on, leaving those on the train the choice of staying where they were until the storm abated or going on foot to their destination."

"Not really!"

"Yes, indeed. Such things happened quite frequently. Then there are stories of terrible gales when the snow piled up on the track until the engine had to be dug out, for snow plows did not keep the tracks clear then as they do now; nor was it an uncommon thing for the mud from the spring washouts to submerge the rails, in which case the engines had to be pulled out of the mire by oxen. In fact, at certain seasons of the year some trains carried oxen for this very purpose. For you must remember that the engines of that date were not powerful enough to make progress through mud, snow, or against fierce head winds. Often a strong gale would delay them for hours or bring them to a standstill altogether."

"Well, I guess it is no wonder we were not equipped to build a trans-continental road under such conditions," said the lad, with a quiet smile.

"Oh, these defects were only a minor part of our railroad tribulations," responded his father. "For example, when Pennsylvania started her first railroad the year after the line between New York and Schenectady was laid, there was a fresh chapter of obstacles. Strangely enough, the locomotive, 'Old Ironsides,' was built by Mr. M. W. Baldwin, whose name has since become celebrated as the founder of the Baldwin Locomotive Works. In 1832, however, the Baldwin locomotive was quite a different product from the present-day magnificently constructed steam engine. This initial attempt at locomotive building was a queer little engine with wheels so light that unless there was plenty of ballast aboard it was impossible to keep it on the track; and besides that, the poor wee thing could not get up steam enough to start itself and in consequence Mr. Baldwin and some of his machinists were obliged to give it a violent push whenever it set out and then leap aboard when it was under way in order to weigh it down and keep it on the track."

"Imagine having to hold an engine down!" ejaculated Steve, with amusement.

"The story simply goes to prove how much in the making locomotives really were," Mr. Tolman said. "And not only did this toy engine have to be started by a friendly push, but it was too feeble to generate steam fast enough to keep itself going after it was once on its way. Therefore every now and then the power would give out and Mr. Baldwin and his men would be forced to get out and run along beside the train, pushing it as they went that it might keep up its momentum until a supply of steam could again be acquired. Can you ask for anything more primitive than that?"

"It certainly makes one realize the progress locomotive builders have made," the boy replied, with gravity.

"It certainly does," agreed his father. "Think how Baldwin and his men must have struggled first with one difficulty and then with another; think how they must have experimented and worked to perfect the tiny engine with which they began! It was the conquering of this multitude of defects that gave to the world the intricate, exquisitely made machine which at this very minute is pulling you and me into New York."

There was an interval of silence during which Stephen glanced out at the flying panorama framed by the window.

"Where was New England all this time?" demanded he, with jealous concern. "Didn't Massachusetts do anything except build the old granite road at Quincy?"

"Railroads, for various reasons, were not popular in Massachusetts," returned his father. "As usual New England was conservative and was therefore slow in waking up to the importance of steam transportation. Boston was on the coast, you see, and had its ships as well as the canal boats that connected the city with the manufacturing districts of the Merrimac. Therefore, although the question of building railroads was agitated in 1819 nothing was done about the matter. As was natural the canal company opposed the venture, and there was little enthusiasm elsewhere concerning a project that demanded a great outlay of money with only scant guarantee that any of it would ever come back to the capitalists who advanced it. Moreover, the public in general was sceptical about railroads or else totally uninterested in them. And even had a railroad been built at this time it would not have been a steam road for it was proposed to propel the cars by horse power just as those at Quincy had been."

"Oh!" interjected Steve scornfully. "They might at least have tried steam."

"People had little faith in it," explained Mr. Tolman. "Those who had the faith lacked the money to back the enterprise, and those who had the money lacked the faith. If a company could have gone ahead and built a steam railroad that was an unquestioned success many persons would undoubtedly have been convinced of its value and been willing to put capital into it; but as matters stood, there was so much antagonism against the undertaking that nobody cared to launch the venture. There were many business men who honestly regarded a steam railroad as a menace to property and so strong was this feeling that in 1824 the town of Dorchester, a village situated a short distance from Boston, actually took legal measures to prevent any railroad from passing through its territory."

"They needn't have been so fussed," said Stephen, with a grin. "Railroads weren't plenty enough to worry them!"

"Oh, the Quincy road was not the only railroad in Massachusetts," his father asserted quickly, "for in spite of opposition a railroad to Lowell, modeled to some extent after the old granite road, had been built. This railroad was constructed on stone ties, as the one at Quincy had been; for although such construction was much more costly it was thought at the time to be far more durable. Several years afterward, when experience had demonstrated that wood possessed more *give*, and that a hard, unyielding roadbed only creates jar, the granite ties that had cost so much were taken up and replaced by wooden ones."

"What a shame!"

"Thus do we live and learn," said his father whimsically. "Our blunders are often very expensive. The only redeeming thing about them is that we pass our experience on to others and save them from tumbling into the same pit. Thus it was with the early railroad builders. When the Boston and Providence Road was constructed this mistake was not repeated and a flexible wooden roadbed was laid. In the meantime a short steam railroad line had been built from Boston to Newton, a distance of seven miles, and gradually the road to this suburb was lengthened until it extended first to Natick and afterward to Worcester, a span of forty-four miles. Over this road, during fine weather, three trains ran daily; in winter there were but two. I presume nothing simpler or less pretentious could have been found than this early railroad whose trains were started at the ringing of a bell hung on a near-by tree. Although it took three hours to make a trip now made in one, the journey was considered very speedy, and unquestionably it was if travelers had to cover the distance by stagecoach. When we consider that in 1834 it took freight the best part of a week to get to Boston by wagons a three-hour trip becomes a miracle."

"I suppose there was not so much freight in those days anyway," Steve speculated.

"Fortunately not. People had less money and less leisure to travel, and therefore there were not so many trunks to be carried; I am not sure, too, but the frugal Americans of that day had fewer clothes to take with them when they did go. Then, as each town or district was of necessity more or less isolated, people knew fewer persons outside of their own communities, did a less extensive business, and had less incentive to go a-visiting. Therefore, although the Boston and Worcester Railroad could boast only two baggage cars (or burthen cars, as they were called), the supply was sufficient, which was fortunate, especially since the freight house in Boston was only large enough to shelter these two."

"And out of all this grew the Boston and Albany Railroad?" questioned the boy.

"Yes, although it was not until 1841, about eight years later, that the line was extended to New York State. By that time tracks had been laid through the Berkshire hills, opening up the western part of Massachusetts. The story of that first momentous fifteen-hour journey of the Boston officials to the New York capital, where they were welcomed and entertained by the Albany dignitaries, is picturesque reading indeed. One of the party who set out from Boston on that memorable day carried with him some spermaceti candles which on the delegates' arrival were burned with great ceremony at the evening dinner."

"I suppose it seemed a wonderful thing to reach Albany in fifteen hours," remarked Steve.

"It was like a fairy tale," his father answered. "To estimate the marvel to the full you must think how long it would have taken to drive the distance, or make the journey by water. Therefore the Boston officials burned their spermaceti candles in triumph; and the next day, when the Albany hosts returned to Boston with their guests, they symbolized the onrush of the world's progress by bringing with them a barrel of flour which had been cut, threshed, and ground only two days before, and put into a wooden barrel made from a tree which was cut down, sawed, and put together while the flour was being ground. This does not seem to us anything very astounding but it was a feat to stop the breath in those days."

"And what did they do with the flour?"

"Oh, that evening when they reached Boston the flour was made into some sort of bread which was served at the dinner the Boston men gave to their visitors."

"I wonder what they would have said if somebody had told them then that sometime people would be going from Boston to New York in five hours?" the lad observed.

"I presume they would not have believed it," was the reply. "Nor would they have been able to credit tales of the great numbers of persons who would constantly be traveling between these two great cities. At that time so few people made the trip that it was very easy to keep track of them; and that they might be identified in case of accident the company retained a list of those who went on the trains. At first this rule worked very well, the passengers being carefully tabulated, together with their place of residence; but later, when traffic began to increase and employees began to have more to do, those whose duty it was to make out these lists became hurried and careless and in the old railroad annals we read such entries as these:

"'Woman in green bonnet; boy; stranger; man with side whiskers,' *etc.*"

A peal of laughter broke from Stephen.

"Railroad officials would have some job to list passengers now, wouldn't they?" he said. "We should all just have to wear identification tags as the men did during the War."

His father acquiesced whimsically.

"I have sometimes feared we might have to come to that, anyway," he replied. "With the sky populated with aeroplanes and the streets filled with automobiles man stands little chance in these days of preserving either his supremacy or his identity. When we get on Fifth Avenue to-day you see if you do not agree with me," he added, as the train pulled into the big station.

CHAPTER VIII

NEW YORK AND WHAT HAPPENED THERE

It took no very long interval to prove that there was some foundation for Mr. Tolman's last assertion, for within a short time the travelers were standing on Fifth Avenue amid the rush of traffic, and feeling of as little importance as dwarfs in a giant's country. The roar of the mighty city, its bustle and confusion, were both exhilarating and terrifying. They had left their luggage at the hotel and now, while Steve's father went to meet a business appointment, the boy was to take a ride up the Avenue on one of the busses, a diversion of which he never tired. To sit on top and look down on the throng in the streets was always novel and entertaining to one who passed his days in a quiet New England town. Therefore he stopped one of the moving vehicles and in great good humor bade his father good-by; and feeling very self-sufficient to be touring New York by himself, clambered eagerly up to a seat.

There were few passengers on the top of the coach for the chill of early morning still lingered in the air; but before they reached Riverside Drive a man with a bright, ruddy countenance and iron-grey hair hailed the bus and climbed up beside the boy. As he took his place he glanced at him kindly and instantly Steve felt a sense of friendliness toward the stranger; and after they had ridden a short distance in silence the man spoke.

"What a beautiful river the Hudson is!" he remarked. "Although I am an old New Yorker I never cease to delight in its charm and its fascinating history. It was on this body of water, you know, that the first steamboat was tried out."

"I didn't know it," Stephen confessed, with an honest blush.

"You will be learning about it some day, I fancy," said the other, with a smile. "An interesting story it is, too. All the beginnings of our great industries and inventions read like romances."

"My father has just been telling me about the beginnings of some of our railroads," observed Steve shyly, "and certainly his stories were as good as fairy tales."

"Is your father especially interested in railroads?" inquired the New Yorker.

"Yes, sir. He is in the railroad business."

"Ah, then that accounts for his filling your ears with locomotives instead of steamboats," declared the man, with a twinkle in his eyes. "Now if I were to spin a yarn for you, it would be of steamboats because that happens to be the thing I am interested in; I believe their history to be one of the most alluring tales to which a boy could listen. Sometime you get a person who knows the drama from start to finish to relate to you the whole marvelous adventure of early steamboating, and you see if it does not beat the railroad story all out."

He laughed a merry laugh in which Stephen joined.

"I wish you would tell it to me yourself," suggested the lad.

The man turned with an expression of pleasure on his red-cheeked face.

"I should like nothing better, my boy," he said quickly, "but you see it is a long story and I am getting out at the next corner.

Sometime, however, we may meet again. Who knows? And if we do you shall hold me to my promise to talk steamboats to you until you cry for mercy."

Bending down he took up a leather bag which he had placed between his feet.

"I am leaving you here, sonny," he said. "I take it you are in New York for a holiday."

"Yes, sir, I am," returned Steve with surprise. "My father and I are staying here just for a few days."

"I hope you will have a jolly good time during your visit," the man said, rising.

Stephen murmured his thanks and watched the erect figure descend from the coach and disappear into a side street. It was not until the New Yorker was well out of sight and the omnibus on its way that his eye was caught by the red bill book lying on the floor at his feet. None of the few scattered passengers had noticed it and stooping, he picked it up and quietly slipped it into his pocket.

What should he do with it?

Of course he could hand it over to the driver of the bus and tell him he had found it. But the man might not be honest and instead of turning it in to the company might keep it. There was little doubt in Steve's mind that the pocketbook belonged to the stranger who had just vacated the place and it was likely his address was inside it. If so, what a pleasure it would be to return the lost article to its rightful owner himself. By so doing he would not only be sure the pocketbook reached its destination but he might see the steamboat man again.

He longed to open the bill book and investigate its contents. What was in it, he wondered. Well, the top of a Fifth Avenue coach was no place to be looking through pocketbooks, there was no question about that. Let alone the fact that persons might be watching him, there was danger that in the fresh morning breeze something might take wing, sail down to the Hudson, and never be seen again. Therefore he decided to curb his impatience and wait until he reached a more favorable spot to examine his suddenly acquired treasure. Accordingly he tucked the long red wallet farther down into the breast pocket of his ulster, and feeling assured that nothing could be done about it at present, gave himself up to the pleasure and excitement of the drive.

It was not until he had rejoined his father at the hotel and the two were sitting at lunch in the great dining room that the thought of it again flashed into his mind.

"Gee, Dad!" he suddenly exclaimed, looking up from his plateful of fried chicken with fork suspended in mid-air. "I meant to tell you I found a pocketbook in the bus this morning."

"A pocketbook!"

"Yes, sir. I think the man who had been sitting beside me must have dropped it when he stooped over to get his bag. At any rate it was lying there after he got out."

"What did you do with it?" Mr. Tolman inquired with no great warmth of interest. "Gave it to the conductor, I suppose."

The boy shook his head.

"No, I didn't," was the answer. "I was afraid he might not turn it in, and as I liked the man who lost it I wanted to be sure he got it, so I brought it back with me."

"And where is it now?" demanded Mr. Tolman, now all attention. "I hope you were not so careless as to leave it upstairs in our room."

"No. I didn't leave it in the room," returned the lad. "It is out in my coat pocket. I meant to take it out and see what was in it; but so many things happened that I forgot about it until this very minute."

"You don't mean that you left it in your ulster pocket and let them hang it out there on the rack?"

"Yes."

"You checked your coat and left it there?"

"Why—yes," came the faltering reply.

Mr. Tolman was on his feet.

"Wait here until I come back," he said in a sharp tone.

"Where are you going?"

"Give me your check quickly," went on his father, without heeding the question. "Hurry!"

Steve fumbled in his jacket pocket.

"Be quick, son, be quick!" commanded Mr. Tolman impatiently. "Don't you know it is never safe to leave anything of value in your coat when you are staying at a large city hotel? Somebody may have taken the pocketbook already."

Scarlet with consternation the lad produced the check.

"If nothing has happened to that pocketbook you will be very fortunate," asserted the man severely. "Stay here! I will be right back."

With beating heart the boy watched him thread his way between the tables and disappear from the dining room into the lobby.

Suppose the bill book should be gone!

What if there had been valuable papers in it, money—a great deal of money—and now through his carelessness it had all disappeared? How stupid he had been not to remember about it and give it to his father the instant they had met! In fact, he would much better have taken a chance and handed it to the bus conductor than to have done the foolish thing he had. He had meant so well and blundered so grievously! How often his father had cautioned him to be careful of money when he was traveling!

Tensely he sat in his chair and waited with miserable anxiety, his eyes fixed on the dining-room door. Then presently, to his great relief, he saw his father returning.

"Did you—" he began.

"You will have to come yourself, Steve," said the elder man whose brow was wrinkled into a frown of annoyance. "The maid who checked the coats is not there, and the one who is insists that the ulster is not mine, and in spite of the check will not allow me to search the pockets of it."

Stephen jumped up.

"I suppose she is right, too," went on Mr. Tolman breathlessly, "but the delay is very unfortunate."

They made their way into the corridor, where by this time an office clerk and another man had joined the maid who was in charge of the coat rack.

Stephen presented his check and without comment the woman handed him his coat. With trembling hand he dived into the deep pocket and from it drew forth the red bill book which he gave to his father.

"There it is, Dad, safe and sound!" he gasped.

Instantly the clerk was in their path.

"I beg pardon, sir," said he with deference, "but does that pocketbook belong to you?"

Mr. Tolman wheeled about.

"Eh—what did you say?" he inquired.

"I asked, sir, if that pocketbook was your property?" repeated the clerk.

Mr. Tolman faced his inquisitor.

"What business is that of yours?" he demanded curtly.

"I am sorry, sir, to appear rude," the hotel employee replied, "but we have been asked to be on the lookout for a young lad who rode this morning on one of the Fifth Avenue busses where a valuable pocketbook was lost. Your son tallies so well with the description that—"

"It was I," put in Stephen eagerly, without regard for consequences. "Who wants me?"

With a smile of eagerness he turned, expecting to encounter the genial face of his acquaintance of the morning. Then he would smile, hold out the pocketbook, and they would laugh together as he explained the adventure, and perhaps afterward have luncheon in company.

Instead no familiar form greeted him. On the contrary the slender man who had been standing beside the clerk came forward.

Mr. Tolman sensed the situation in a second.

"You mean somebody thinks my son took the pocketbook?" asked he indignantly, as he confronted the clerk and his companion.

"It is not my affair, sir, and I am sorry it should happen in our hotel," apologized the clerk. "Perhaps if you will just explain the whole matter to this gentleman—" he broke off, saying in an undertone to the man at his elbow. "This is your boy, Donovan."

The tall man came nearer.

"You are a detective?" asked Mr. Tolman bluntly.

"Well, something of the sort, sir," admitted the man called Donovan. "It is occasionally my business to hunt people up."

"And you have been sent to hunt my son up?"

Donovan nodded.

Stephen turned white and his father put a reassuring hand on his shoulder.

"My son and I," he replied, addressing the detective quietly, "can explain this entire affair to you and will do so gladly. The boy did find the pocketbook but he was ignorant of its value because he has not even looked inside it. In fact, that he had the article in his possession did not come into his mind until a few moments ago. If he had known the thing was valuable, do you suppose he would have left it in his ulster pocket and checked the coat in a public place like this?"

The detective made no reply.

"We both shall be very glad," went on Mr. Tolman firmly, "to go with you to headquarters and straighten the matter out."

"There may be no need of that, sir," Donovan responded with a pleasant smile. "If we can just talk the affair over in a satisfactory way—"

"Suppose you come upstairs to our room," suggested Mr. Tolman. "That will give us more quiet and privacy. Will that be agreeable to you?"

"Perfectly."

As the three walked toward the elevator Steve glanced with trepidation at the plain-clothes man.

The boy knew he had done nothing wrong; but would he be able to convince the detective of the truth of his story? He was thoroughly frightened and wondered whether his father was also alarmed.

If, however, Mr. Tolman was worried he at least did not show it. Instead he courteously led the way from the elevator down the dim corridor and unlocked the door of Number 379.

"Come in, Mr. Donovan," he said cordially. "Here is a chair and a cigar. Now, son, tell us the story of this troublesome pocketbook from beginning to end."

In a trembling voice Stephen began his tale. He spoke slowly, uncertainly, for he was well scared. Gradually, however, he forgot his agitation and his voice became more positive. He recounted the details of the omnibus ride with great care, adding ingenuously when he came to the termination of the narrative:

"And I hoped the man's name would be inside the pocketbook because I liked him very much and wanted to return to him what he had lost."

"And wasn't it?" put in Mr. Donovan quickly.

"I don't know," was the innocent retort. "Don't you remember I told you that I hadn't looked inside yet?"

The detective laughed with satisfaction.

"That was a shabby trick of mine, youngster," said he. "It was mean to try to trap you."

"Trap me?" repeated Steve vaguely.

"There, there, sonny!" went on Donovan kindly. "Don't you worry a minute more about this mix-up. Mr. Ackerman, the gentleman who lost the bill book, did not think for a second that you had taken it. He simply was so sure that he had lost it on the bus that he wanted to locate you and find out whether you knew anything about it or not. His name was not inside the pocketbook, you see, and therefore any one who found it would have no way of tracing its owner. What it contains are valuable papers and a big wad of Liberty Bonds which, as your father knows, could quickly be converted into cash. In consequence Mr. Ackerman decided that the sooner the pocketbook was found the better. The omnibus people denied any knowledge of it and you were the only remaining clue."

Mr. Tolman sank back in his chair and a relaxation of his muscles betrayed for the first time that he had been much more disturbed than he had appeared to be.

"Well," he said, lighting a fresh cigar, "the bill book is not only located but we can hand it back intact to its owner. If you can inform us where the gentleman lives, my boy and I will call a taxi and go to his house or office with his property."

A flush of embarrassment suffused the face of the officer.

"Maybe you would like to come with us, Donovan," added Mr. Tolman, who instantly interpreted the man's confusion.

"I hate to be dogging your footsteps, sir, in this fashion," Mr. Donovan answered, with obvious sincerity. "Still, I—"

"You have your orders, no doubt."

"Well, yes, sir," admitted the plain-clothes man with reluctance. "I have."

"You were to keep your eye on us until the pocketbook reached its owner."

"That's about it, sir. Not that I personally have the least suspicion that a gentleman like you would—"

"That is all right, my man. I perfectly understand your position," Mr. Tolman cut in. "After all, you have your duty to do and business is business. We'll just telephone Mr. Ackerman that we are coming so that we shall be sure of catching him, and then we will go right up there."

"Very well, sir."

Stephen's father started toward the telephone and then, as if struck by a sudden thought, paused and turned.

"Steve," he said, "I believe you are the person to communicate with Mr. Ackerman. Call him up and tell him you have found his purse and that you and your father would like to come up to his house, if it will be convenient, and return it."

"All right, Dad."

"You will find his number on this slip of paper, sonny," the detective added, handing the lad a card. "He is not at his office.

He went home to lunch in the hope that he had left the pocketbook there."

After some delay Stephen succeeded in getting the number written on the card. A servant answered the summons.

"May I speak to Mr. Ackerman, please?" inquired the lad. "He is at luncheon? No, it would not do the least good for me to tell you my name for he would not know who it was. Just tell him that the boy who sat beside him this morning on the Fifth Avenue bus—" there was a little chuckle. "Oh, he will be here directly, will he? I thought perhaps he would."

A moment later a cheery voice which Steve at once recognized to be that of the steamboat man came over the wire:

"Well, sonny?"

"I found your bill book, Mr. Ackerman, and my father and I would like to bring it up to you."

"Well, well! that is fine news!" cried the man at the other end of the line. "How did you know who it belonged to?"

"Oh, I—we—found out—my father and I," stammered the lad. "May we come up to your house with it now?"

"You would much better let me come to you; then only one person will be inconvenienced," the New Yorker returned pleasantly. "Where are you staying?"

"At the Manhattan."

"You must not think of taking the trouble of coming way up here. Let me join you and your father at your hotel."

"Very well, Mr. Ackerman. If you'd rather—"

"I certainly should rather!" was the emphatic answer. "I could not think of bringing two people so far out of their way."

"There are three of us!" squeaked Stephen.

"Three?"

"Yes, sir. We have another person—a friend—with us,"

explained the boy, with quiet enjoyment. How easy it was to laugh now!

"All the more reason why I should come to you, then," asserted Mr. Ackerman. "I will be at the Manhattan within half an hour. Perhaps if you and your father and your friend have the afternoon free you would like to go to some sort of a show with me after we conclude our business. Since you are here on a holiday you can't be very busy."

Stephen's eyes sparkled with merriment.

"I don't know whether our friend can go or not," he replied politely, "but I think perhaps Dad and I could; and if we can we should like to very much."

"That will be excellent. I will come right along. Not only shall I be glad to get my pocketbook back again but I shall be glad to see you once more. I told you this morning that I had a feeling we should meet some time. Whom shall I ask for at the hotel?"

"Stephen Tolman."

With a click the boy hung up the receiver.

"Mr. Ackerman is coming right down," said he, addressing his father and the detective with a mischievous smile. "He has invited the three of us to go to the matinee with him."

"The three of us!" echoed the plain-clothes man.

"Yes," returned the lad. "I told him we had a friend with us and so he said to bring him along."

"Good heavens!" Donovan ejaculated.

Mr. Tolman laughed heartily.

"Not all the thieves you arrest take you to a theater party afterward, do they, Officer?" he asked.

"I said from the first you were gentlemen," Mr. Donovan asserted with humor.

"But couldn't you go?" inquired Steve, quite seriously.

"Bless you, no, sonny!" replied the man. "I am from head-quarters, you know, and my work is chasing up crooks—not going to matinees."

Nevertheless there was an intonation of gentleness in his voice, as he added, "I am obliged to you just the same, for in spite of my calling I am a human being and I appreciate being treated like one."

CHAPTER IX

AN ASTOUNDING CALAMITY

Mr. Ackerman was as good as his word, for within half an hour he presented himself at the hotel where he found Mr. Tolman, Mr. Donovan and Steve awaiting him in their pleasant upstairs room. As he joined them his eye traveled inquiringly from one to another of the group and lingered with curiosity on the face of the detective. The next instant he was holding out his hand to Stephen.

"Well, my boy, I am glad to see you again," said he, a ring of heartiness in his voice.

"And I am glad to see you, too, Mr. Ackerman," Steve replied, returning the hand-clasp with fervor. "This is my father, sir; and this"—for a second he hesitated, then continued, "is our friend, Mr. Donovan."

With cordiality the New Yorker acknowledged the introductions.

"Mr. Donovan," explained Mr. Tolman, scanning Mr. Ackerman's countenance with a keen, half-quizzical expression, "is from headquarters."

The steamboat magnate started and shot a quick glance at those present. It was plain he was disconcerted and uncertain as to how to proceed.

Mr. Donovan, however, came to his rescue, stepping tactfully into the breach:

"I was not needed for anything but to supply your address, sir; but I was able to do that, so between us all we have contrived to return your pocketbook to you as good as before it left your possession."

As he spoke Mr. Tolman drew forth the missing bill book and held it toward its owner.

"That looks pretty good to me!" Mr. Ackerman exclaimed, as he took the article from Mr. Tolman's outstretched hand and regarded it reflectively. "I don't know when I have ever done anything so careless and stupid. You see I had got part way to the bank before I remembered that I had left my glasses, on which I am absolutely dependent, at home. Therefore, there being no taxi in sight, I hailed a passing bus and climbed up beside this youngster. How the bill book happened to slip out of my pocket I cannot explain. It seemed to me it would be safer to have the securities upon my person than in a bag that might be snatched from me; but apparently my logic was at fault. I was, however, so certain of my wisdom that I never thought to question it until I had reached the sidewalk and the bus had gone.

"Your boy, Mr. Tolman, confided while we rode along this morning that he was visiting in New York for a few days; but of course I did not ask his name or address and so when I wanted his help in tracing the missing pocketbook I had no way of locating him beyond assuming that he must be staying at one of the hotels. Therefore when the omnibus company could furnish no clue, I got into touch with an agency whose business it is to hunt people up. If the pocketbook had been dropped on the bus I felt sure your boy, who was almost the only other person on top of the coach, would know about it; if, on the other hand, it had been dropped in the street, my problem would be a different one. In either case the sooner I knew my course of action the better. I hope you will believe, Mr. Tolman, that when I called in the aid of detectives I had no suspicions against your son's honesty."

Mr. Tolman waved the final remark aside good-humoredly.

"We have not taken the affair as a personal matter at all," he declared. "We fully appreciate your difficulty in finding Stephen, for he was also up against the problem of finding you. New York is a rather large city anyway, and for two people who do not even know one another's names to get together is like hunting a needle in a haystack. Our only recourse to discovering the owner of the pocketbook would be through the advertising columns of the papers and that is the method we should have followed had not Donovan appeared and saved us the trouble."

He exchanged a smile with the detective.

"The advertising column was my one hope," Mr. Ackerman replied. "I felt sure that any honest person who picked up the purse would advertise it. It was not the honest people I was worrying about. It was the thought that I had dropped the bill book in the street where any Tom-Dick-and-Harry could run away with it that concerned me. Moreover, even if your boy had found it on the bus, he might have turned it in to an employee of the coach line who was not honest enough to give it in turn to his superiors. So I wanted to know where I stood; and now that I do I cannot tell you how grateful I am both to Stephen and to this officer here for the service they have rendered me." Then, turning toward Mr. Tolman, he added in an undertone, "I hope neither you nor your son have suffered any annoyance through this unfortunate incident."

"Not in the least," was the prompt response. "I confess we

were a trifle disconcerted at first; but Mr. Donovan has performed his duty with such courtesy that we entertain toward him nothing but gratitude."

"I am glad of that," Mr. Ackerman replied, "for I should deeply regret placing either you or your boy, even for a moment, in an uncomfortable position, or one where it might appear that I—"

But Mr. Tolman cut him short.

"You took the quickest, most sensible course, Ackerman," said he. "Too much was at stake for you to risk delay. When a pocketbook filled with negotiable securities disappears one must of necessity act with speed. Neither Stephen nor I cherish the least ill-will about the affair; do we, son?"

"No, indeed."

Then smiling ingenuously up into the face of the New York man, he said:

"Don't you want to look in your pocketbook and see if everything is all right, sir?"

The steamboat financier laughed.

"You are a prudent young man," declared he. "No, I am quite willing to risk that the property you have so kindly guarded is intact."

"It ought to be," the boy said. "I haven't even opened the pocketbook."

"A better proof still that everything is safe within it," chuckled Mr. Ackerman. "No, sonny, I am not worrying. I should not worry even if you had ransacked the bill book from one end to the other. I'd take a chance on the honesty of a boy like you."

Mr. Tolman, however, who had been listening, now came forward and broke into the conversation:

"Stephen's suggestion is a good, businesslike one, Ackerman," he declared. "As a mere matter of form—not as a slam against our morals—I am sure that both he and I would prefer that you examined your property while we are all here together and assure yourself that it is all right."

"Pooh! Pooh! Nonsense!" objected the financier.

"It is a wise notion, Mr. Ackerman," rejoined Mr. Donovan. "Business is business. None of us questions the honor of Mr. Tolman or his son. They know that. Nevertheless I am sure we should all feel better satisfied if you went through the formality of an investigation."

"Very well, just as you say. But I want it understood that I do it at their and your request. I am perfectly satisfied to leave things as they are."

Taking the now familiar red pocketbook from his coat he opened it unconcernedly; then the three persons watching him saw a look of consternation banish the smile from his face.

"What's wrong, Ackerman?" inquired the plain-clothes man quickly.

Without a word the other held the bill book toward him. It was empty. Bonds, securities, money were gone! A gasp of incredulity came from Stephen.

"I didn't open it—truly I didn't!" exclaimed he, in a terror-stricken voice.

But Mr. Ackerman did not heed the remark.

"I am afraid this looks pretty black for us, Ackerman," said Mr. Tolman slowly. "We have nothing to give you but the boy's word."

Mr. Donovan, however, who had been studying the group with a hawklike scrutiny now sprang to his feet and caught up his hat.

"I don't see how they dared put it over!" he exclaimed excitedly. "But they almost got away with it. Even I was fooled."

"You don't mean to insinuate," Mr. Tolman burst out, "that you think we—"

"Good heavens, no!" replied the detective with his hand on the door knob. "Don't go getting hot under the collar, Mr. Tolman. Nobody is slamming *you*. I have been pretty stupid about this affair, I'm afraid; but give me credit for recognizing honest people when I see them. No, somebody has tricked you—tricked you all. But the game isn't up yet. If you gentlemen will just wait here—"

The sentence was cut short by the banging of the door. The detective was gone. His departure was followed by an awkward silence.

Mr. Ackerman's face clouded into a frown of disappointment and anxiety; Mr. Tolman paced the floor and puffed viciously at a cigar; and Steve, his heart cold within him, looked from one to the other, chagrin, mortification and terror in his eyes.

"I didn't open the pocketbook, Mr. Ackerman," he reiterated for the twentieth time. "I truly didn't."

But the steamboat magnate was too deeply absorbed in his own thoughts and speculations to notice the high-pitched voice with its intonation of distress.

At last Mr. Tolman could endure the situation no longer.

"This is a most unfortunate happening, Ackerman," he burst out. "I am more concerned about it than I can express. My boy and I are utter strangers to you and we have no way of proving our honesty. All I can say is that we are as much amazed at the turn affairs have taken as yourself, and we regret it with quite as much poignancy—perhaps more since it reflects directly upon us. If there is anything we can do—"

He stopped, awaiting a reply from the other man, but none came.

"Good heavens, Ackerman," he cried. "You don't mean to say you do not believe my son and me—that you suspect us of double-dealing!"

"I don't know what to believe, Tolman," owned Mr. Ackerman with candor. "I want very much to credit your story; in my heart, I do credit it. But head and heart seem to be at variance in this matter. Frankly I am puzzled to know where the contents of that pocketbook have gone. Were the things taken out before the bill book fell into your son's hands or afterward? And if afterward, who took them? Who had the chance? Donovan seems to think he has a clue, but I confess I have none."

"Hadn't you looked over the bonds and stuff since you took them home?"

"No," Mr. Ackerman admitted. "I got them from the broker yesterday and as it was too late to put them into the safe-deposit vault, I took them home with me instead of putting them in our office safe as I should have done. I thought it would be easier for me to stop at the bank with them this morning on my way to business. It was foolish planning but I aimed to save time."

"So the pocketbook was at your house over night?"

Mr. Ackerman nodded.

"Yes," confessed he. "Nevertheless it did not go out of my possession. I had it in the inner pocket of my coat all the time."

"You are sure no one took the things out while you were asleep last night?"

"Why—I—I don't see how they could," faltered Mr. Ackerman. "My servants are honest—at least, they always have been. I have had them for years. Moreover, none of them knew I had valuable papers about me. How could they?" was the reply.

Once more silence fell upon the room.

"Come, Tolman," ejaculated the steamboat man presently, "you are a level-headed person. What is your theory?"

"If I did not know my son and myself as well as I do," Mr. Tolman answered with deliberation, "my theory would be precisely what I fancy yours is. I should reason that during the interval between the finding of the purse and its return the contents had been extracted."

He saw the New Yorker color.

"That, I admit, is my logical theory," Mr. Ackerman owned with a blush, "but it is not my intuitive one. My brain tells me one thing and my heart another; and in spite of the fact that the arguments of my brain seem correct I find myself believing my heart and in consequence cherishing a groundless faith in you and your boy," concluded he, with a faint smile.

"That is certainly generous of you, Ackerman!" Mr. Tolman returned, much moved by the other's confidence. "Stephen and I are in a very compromising situation with nothing but your belief between us and a great deal of unpleasantness. We appreciate your attitude of mind more than we can express. The only other explanation I can offer, and in the face of the difficulties it would involve it hardly seems a possible one, is that while the coat was hanging in the lobby—"

There was a sound outside and a sharp knock at the door, and an instant later Mr. Donovan entered, his face wreathed in smiles. Following him was the woman who had checked the coats, a much frightened bell boy, and a blue-uniformed policeman.

The woman was sobbing.

"Indeed, sir," she wailed, approaching Steve, "I never meant to keep the pocketbook and make trouble for you. I have a boy of my own at home, a lad about your age. What is to become of him now? Oh, dear; oh, dear!"

She burst into passionate weeping.

"Now see here, my good woman, stop all this crying and talk quietly," cut in the policeman in a curt but not unkind tone. "If you will tell us the truth, perhaps we can help you. In any case we must know exactly what happened."

"She must understand that anything she says can be used against her," cautioned the detective, who in spite of his eagerness to solve the mystery was determined the culprit should have fair play.

"Indeed, I don't care, sir," protested the maid, wiping her eyes on her ridiculously small apron. "I can't be any worse off than I am now with a policeman taking me to the lock-up. I'll tell the gentlemen the truth, I swear I will."

With a courtesy he habitually displayed toward all womanhood Mr. Tolman drew forward a chair and she sank gratefully into it.

"I spied the bill book in the young gentleman's pocket the minute he took off his coat," began she in a low tone. "It was bright colored and as it was sticking part way out I couldn't help seeing it. Of course, I expected he would take it with him into the dining room but when he didn't I came to the conclusion that there couldn't be anything of value in it. But by and by I had more coats to hang up and one of them, a big, heavy, fur-lined one, brushed against the young gentleman's ulster and knocked the pocketbook out on to the floor so that it lay open under the coat rack. It was then that I saw it was stuffed full of papers and things."

She stopped a moment to catch her breath and then went resolutely on:

"It seemed to me it was no sort of a plan to put the wallet back into the lad's pocket, for when I wasn't looking somebody might take it. So I decided I much better keep it safe for him, and maybe," she owned with a blush, "get a good-sized tip for doing it. I have a big pocket in my underskirt where I carry my own money and I slipped it right in there, meaning to hand it to the young man when he came out from lunch."

The corners of her mouth twitched and her tears began to fall again, but she wiped them away with her apron and proceeded steadily:

"But nothing turned out as I planned, for no sooner was the bill book in my pocket than I was called away to help about the wraps at a lady's luncheon upstairs. There were so many people about the hall that I had no chance to restore the bill book to the lad's pocket without some one seeing me and thinking, perhaps, that I was stealing. There was no help but to take it with me, trusting they would not keep me long upstairs and that I would get back to my regular place before the young gentleman came out of the dining room. It was when I got out of the elevator in the upper hall that I spied Dick, one of the bell boys I knew, and I called to him; and after explaining that I couldn't get away to go downstairs I asked him to take the wallet and put it in 47's pocket. He's a good-natured little chap and always ready to do an errand, and more than that he's an honest boy. So I felt quite safe and went to work, supposing the young man had his pocketbook long ago."

All eyes were turned upon the unlucky bell boy who hung his head and colored uncomfortably.

"So it was the boy who took the contents of the pocketbook!" was Mr. Ackerman's comment.

"Speak up, boy," commanded the officer. "The gentleman is talking to you." The lad looked up with a frightened start.

He might have been sixteen years of age but he did not look

it for he was pale and underfed; nor was there anything in his bearing to indicate the poise and maturity of one who was master of the occasion. On the contrary, he was simply a boy who was frankly distressed and frightened, and as unfeignedly helpless in the present emergency as if he had been six years old and been caught stealing jam from the pantry shelf. It did not take more than a glance to convince the onlookers that he was no hardened criminal. If he had done wrong it had been the result either of impulse or mischief, and the dire result of his deed was a thing he had been too unsophisticated to foresee. The plight in which he now found himself plainly amazed and overwhelmed him and he looked pleadingly at his captors.

"Well, my boy, what have you to say for yourself?" repeated Mr. Ackerman more gently.

"Nothin'."

"Nothing?"

"No, sir."

"You did take the things out of the pocketbook then."

"Yes, sir."

"But you are not a boy accustomed to taking what does not belong to you."

The culprit shot a glance of gratitude toward the speaker but made no reply.

"How did you happen to do it this time?" persisted Mr. Ackerman kindly. "Come, tell me all about it."

Perhaps it was the ring of sympathy in the elder man's voice that won the boy's heart. Whatever the charm, it conquered; and he met the eyes that scanned his countenance with a timid smile.

"I wanted to see what was in the pocketbook," said he with naïve honesty, "and so I took the things out to look at them. I wasn't goin' to keep 'em. I dodged into one of the little alcoves in the hall and had just pulled the papers out when I heard somebody comin'. So I crammed the whole wad of stuff into my pocket, waiting for a time when I could look it over and put it back. But I got held up just like Mrs. Nolan did," he pointed toward the woman in the chair. "Some man was sick and the clerk sent me to get a bottle of medicine the minute I got downstairs, and all I had the chance to do was to stick the empty wallet in 47's pocket and beat it for the drug store. I thought there would be letters or something among the papers that would give the name of the man they belonged to, and I'd take 'em to the clerk at the desk an' say I found 'em. But no sooner had I got the medicine up to room Number 792 than the policeman nabbed me with the papers an' things on me. That's all there is to it, sir."

"Have you the things now?" the officer put in quickly.

"Sure! Didn't I just tell you I hadn't had the chance to hand 'em over to the clerk," the boy reiterated, pulling a wad of crumpled Liberty Bonds and documents out of his pocket, and tumbling them upon the table.

There was no doubting the lad's story. Truth spoke in every line of his face and in the frankness with which he met the scrutiny of those who listened to him. If one had questioned his uprightness the facts bore out his statements, for once out of the hotel on an errand he might easily have taken to his heels and never returned; or he might have disposed of his booty during his absence. But he had done neither. He had gone to the drug store and come back with every intention of making restitution for the result of his curiosity. That was perfectly evident.

"I'm sorry, sir," he declared, when no one spoke. "I know I shouldn't have looked in the pocketbook or touched the papers; but I meant no harm—honest I didn't."

"I'll be bound of that, sir," the woman interrupted. "Dick was ever a lad to be trusted. The hotel people will tell you that. He's been here several years and there's never been a thing against him. I blame myself for getting him into this trouble, for without meaning to I put temptation in his way. I know that what he's told you is the living truth, and I pray you'll try and believe him and let him go. If harm was to come to the lad through me I'd never forgive myself. Let the boy go free and put the blame on me, if you must arrest somebody. I'm older and it doesn't so much matter; but it's terrible to start a child of his age in as a criminal. The name will follow him through life. He'll never get rid of it and have a fair chance. Punish me but let the little chap go, I beg of you," pleaded the woman, with streaming eyes.

Mr. Ackerman cleared his throat; it was plain that the simple eloquence of the request had touched him deeply.

"With your permission, officer, I am going to withdraw my charge," he said, with a tremor in his voice. "You are to let both these persons go scot free. You, my good woman, meant well but acted foolishly. As for the boy, Donovan, I will assume the responsibility for him."

"You are willing to stand behind him, Mr. Ackerman?"

"I am."

The detective turned toward the boy who had risen and was fumbling awkwardly with the brass buttons adorning his uniform.

"You hear, Dick Martin, what the gentleman says," began he impressively. "He believes you are a good boy, and as you have handed back the valuables in your possession he is going to take a chance on you and let you go."

A wave of crimson swept over the face of the boy and for the first time the tension in the youthful countenance relaxed.

"But Mr. Ackerman," Donovan continued, "expects you are going to behave yourself in future and never do such a thing again."

"I am going to see your father, Dick," broke in Mr. Ackerman's kindly voice, "and talk with him and—"

"I haven't any father," declared the lad.

"Your mother then."

"I've no mother either."

"Who do you live with?"

"Mr. Aronson."

"Is he a relative?"

"Oh, no, sir! I haven't any relatives. There's nobody belongin' to me. Mr. Aronson is the tailor downstairs where I sleep. When I ain't working here I do errands for him and he lets me have a cot in a room with four other boys—newsboys, bell hops and the like. We pay two dollars between us for the room and sometimes when I carry a lot of boxes round for Mr. Aronson he gives me my breakfast."

"Nobody else is responsible for you?"

"Nop!" returned the boy with emphasis. "No, sir, I mean."

"I'll attend to all this, Donovan," murmured Mr. Ackerman in an undertone to the detective. "The lad shall not remain there. I don't know yet just what I'll do with him but I will plan something." Then addressing the lad, he continued, "In the meantime, Dick, you are to consider me your relative. Later I shall hunt you up and we will get better acquainted. Be a good boy, for I expect some day you are going to make me very proud of you."

"What!"

In sheer astonishment the boy regarded his benefactor.

There was something very appealing in the little sharp-featured face which had now lost much of its pallor and softened into friendliness.

"Why shouldn't you make me proud of you?" inquired Mr. Ackerman softly. "You can, you know, if you do what is right."

"I'm goin' to try to, sir," burst out Dick with earnestness. "I'm goin' to try to with all my might."

"That is all any one can ask of you, sonny," replied the steamboat magnate. "Come, shake hands. Remember, I believe in you, and shall trust you to live up to your word. The officer is going to let you go and none of us is going to mention what has happened. I will fix up everything for you and Mrs. Nolan so you can both go back to your work without interference. Now bid Mr. Tolman and his son good-by and run along. Before I leave the hotel I will look you up and you can give me Mr. Aronson's address."

Master Richard Martin needed no second bidding. Eager to be gone he awkwardly put out his hand, first to Mr. Tolman and then to Steve; and afterward, with a shy smile to the detective and the policeman and a boyish duck of his head, he shot into the hall and they heard him rushing pell-mell down the corridor. Mrs. Nolan, however, was more self-controlled. She curtsied elaborately to each of the men and called down upon their heads every blessing that the sky could rain, and it was only after her breath had become quite exhausted that she consented to retire from the room and in company with the policeman and the detective proceeded downstairs in the elevator.

"Well, Tolman," began the New Yorker when they were at last alone, "you see my heart was my best pilot. I put faith in it and it led me aright. Unfortunately it is now too late for the matinee but may I not renew my invitation and ask you and your son to dine with me this evening and conclude our eventful day by going to the theater afterward?"

Mr. Tolman hesitated.

"Don't refuse," pleaded the steamboat man. "Our acquaintance has, I confess, had an unfortunate beginning; but a bad beginning makes for a good ending, they say, and I feel sure the old adage will prove true in our case. Accept my invitation and let us try it out."

"You are very kind," murmured Mr. Tolman vaguely, "but I—"

"Help me to persuade your father to be generous, Stephen," interposed Mr. Ackerman. "We must not let a miserable affair like this break up what might, perhaps, have been a delightful friendship."

"I don't need any further persuading, Ackerman," Mr. Tolman spoke quickly. "I accept your invitation with great pleasure."

"That's right!" cried Mr. Ackerman, with evident gratification. "Suppose you come to my house at seven o'clock if that will be convenient for you. We will have a pleasant evening together and forget lost pocketbooks, detectives and policemen."

Taking out a small card, he hurriedly scrawled an address upon it.

"I keep a sort of bachelor's hall out on Riverside Drive," explained he, with a shade of wistfulness. "My butler looks out for me and sees that I do not starve to death. He and his son are really excellent housekeepers and make me very comfortable." He slipped into his overcoat. "At seven, then," he repeated. "Don't fail me for I should be much disappointed. Good-by!" and with a wave of his hand he departed, leaving Stephen and his father to themselves.

CHAPTER X

AN EVENING OF ADVENTURE

That evening Steve and his father took a taxi-cab and drove to the number Mr. Ackerman had given them. It proved to be an imposing apartment house of cream brick overlooking the Hudson; and the view from the fifth floor, where their host lived, was such a fascinating one that the boy could hardly be persuaded to leave the bay window that fronted the shifting panorama before him.

"So you like my moving picture, do you, Steve?" inquired the New Yorker merrily.

"It is great! If I lived here I shouldn't do a bit of studying," was the lad's answer.

"You think the influence of the place bad, then."

"It would be for me," Stephen chuckled.

Both Mr. Tolman and Mr. Ackerman laughed.

"I will own," the latter confessed, "that at first those front windows demoralized me not a little. They had the same lure for me as they have for you. But by and by I gained the strength of mind to turn my back and let the Hudson River traffic look out for itself."

"You might try that remedy, son," suggested Steve's father.

"No, no, Tolman! Let the boy alone. If he is enjoying the ferries and steamboats so much the better."

"But there seem to be plenty of steamboats here in the room to enjoy," was Mr. Tolman's quick retort.

"Steamboats?" repeated Steve vaguely, turning and looking about him.

Sure enough, there were steamboats galore! Wherever he looked he saw them. Not only were the walls covered with pictures of every imaginable type of steamer, but wherever there was space enough there were tiers of little ship models in glass cases. There were side-wheelers, awkwardly constructed boats with sprawling paddles, screw propellers, and twin-screw craft; ferryboats, tugs, steam yachts, and ocean liners. Every known variety of sea-going contrivance was represented. The large room was like a museum of ships and the boy gave an involuntary exclamation of delight.

"Jove!"

It was a laconic tribute to the marvels about him but it was uttered with so much vehemence that there was no mistaking its sincerity. Evidently, terse as it was, its ring of fervor satisfied Mr. Ackerman for he smiled to himself.

"I never saw so many boats in all my life!" burst out Steve.

"I told you I was in the steamboat business," put in Mr. Ackerman mischievously.

"I should think you were!" was the lad's comment.

"This is a wonderful collection, Ackerman," Mr. Tolman asserted, as he rose and began to walk about the room. "How did you ever get it together? Many of these prints are priceless."

"Oh, I have been years doing it," Mr. Ackerman said. "It has been my hobby. I have chosen to sink my money in these toys instead of in an abandoned farm or antique furniture. It is just a matter of taste, you see."

"You must have done some scouring of the country to make

your collection so complete. I don't see how you ever succeeded in finding these old pictures and models. It is a genuine history lesson."

"I do not deserve all the credit, by any means," the capitalist protested with modesty. "My grandfather, who was one of the owners of the first of the Hudson River steamers, began collecting pictures and drawings; and at his death they came to my father who added to them. Afterward, when the collection descended to me, I tried to fill in the gaps in order to make the sequence complete. Of course in many cases I have not been able to find what I wanted, for neither prints nor models of some of the ships I desired were to be had. Either there were no copies of them in existence, or if there were no money could tempt their owners to part with them. Still I have a well enough graded lot to show the progression."

"I should think you had!" said Mr. Tolman heartily. "You have arranged them beautifully, too, from the old whalers and early American coasting ships to the clippers. Then come the first steam packets, I see, and then the development of the steamboat through its successive steps up to our present-day floating palace. It tells its own story, doesn't it?"

"In certain fashion, yes," Mr. Ackerman agreed. "But the real romance of it will never be fully told, I suppose. What an era of progress through which to have lived!"

"And shared in, as your family evidently did," interposed Mr. Tolman quickly.

His host nodded.

"Yes," he answered, "I am quite proud to think that both my father and my grandfather had their humble part in the story."

"And well you may be. They were makers of history."

Both men were silent an instant, each occupied with his own thoughts.

Mr. Tolman moved reflectively toward the mantelpiece before which Steve was standing, gazing intently at a significant quartette of tiny models under glass. First came a ship of graceful outline, having a miniature figurehead of an angel at its prow and every sail set. Beside this was an ungainly side-wheeler with scarce a line of beauty to commend it. Next in order came an exquisite, up-to-date ocean liner; and the last in the group was a modern battle-ship with guns, wireless, and every detail cunningly reproduced.

Stephen stood speechless before them.

"What are you thinking of, son?" his father asked.

"Why, I—" the boy hesitated.

"Come, tell us! I'd like to know, too," echoed Mr. Ackerman.

"Why, to be honest I was wondering how you happened to pick these particular four for your mantel," replied the lad with confusion.

The steamboat man smiled kindly.

"You think there are handsomer boats in the room than these, do you?"

"Certainly there are better looking steamships than this one," Steve returned, pointing with a shrug of his shoulders at the clumsy side-wheeler.

"But that rather ugly craft is the most important one of the lot, my boy," Mr. Tolman declared.

"I suppose that is true," Mr. Ackerman agreed. "The fate of all the others hung on that ship."

"Why?" was the boy's prompt question.

"Oh, it is much too long a yarn to tell you now," laughed his host. "Were we to begin that tale we should not get to the theater to-night, say nothing of having any dinner."

"I'd like to hear the story," persisted Stephen.

"You will be reading it from a book some day."

"I'd rather hear you tell it."

"If that isn't a spontaneous compliment, Ackerman, I don't know what is," laughed Mr. Tolman.

The steamboat man did not reply but he could not quite disguise his pleasure, although he said a bit gruffly:

"We shall have to leave the story and go to the show to-night. I've bought the tickets and there is no escape," added he humorously. "But perhaps before you leave New York there will be some other chance for me to spin my yarn for you, and put your father's railroad romances entirely in the shade."

The butler announced dinner and they passed into the dining room.

If, however, Stephen thought that he was now to leave ships behind him he was mistaken, for the dining room proved to be quite as much of a museum as the library had been. Against the dull blue paper hung pictures of racing yachts, early American fighting ships, and nautical encounters on the high seas. The house was a veritable wonderland, and so distracted was the lad that he could scarcely eat.

"Come, come, son," objected Mr. Tolman at last, "you will not be ready in time to go to any show unless you turn your attention to your dinner."

"That's right," Mr. Ackerman said. "Fall to and eat your roast beef. We are none too early as it is."

Accordingly Stephen fixed his eyes on his plate with resolution and tried his best to think no more of his alluring surroundings. With the coming of the ice-cream he had almost forgotten there were such things as ships, and when he rose from the table he found himself quite as eager to set forth to the theater as any other healthy-minded lad of his age would have been.

The "show" Mr. Ackerman had selected had been chosen with much care and was one any boy would have delighted to see. The great stage had, for the time being, been transformed to a western prairie and across it came a group of canvas-covered wagons, or prairie schooners, such as were used in the early days by the first settlers of the West. Women and children were huddled beneath the arched canopy of coarse cloth and inside this shelter they passed the weary days and nights of travel. Through sun and storm the wagons rumbled on; jogging across the rough, uncharted country and jolting over rocks, sagebrush, and sand. There were streams to ford, mountains to climb on the long trip westward, but undaunted by obstacles the heroic little band of settlers who had with such determination left kin and comfort behind them passed on to that new land toward which their faces were set.

It was such a company as this that Stephen now saw pictured before him. Perched on the front seat of the wagon driving the horses was the father of the family, rugged, alert, and of the woodsman type characteristic of the New England pioneer. The cavalcade halted. A fire was built and the travelers cooked their supper. Across the valley one could see the fading sunset deepen into twilight. From a little stream near-by the men brought water for the tired horses. Then the women and children clambered into the "ship of the desert" and prepared for a night's rest.

In the meantime the men lingered about the dying fire and one of them, a gun in his hand, paced back and forth as if on guard. Then suddenly he turned excitedly to his comrades with his finger on his lips. He had heard a sound, the sound they all dreaded,—the cry of an Indian.

Presently over the crest of the hill came stealing a stealthy band of savages. On they came, crouching against the rocks and moving forward with the lithe, gliding motion of serpents. The men sank down behind the brush, weapons in hand, and waited. On came the bloodthirsty Indians. Then, just when the destruction of the travelers seemed certain, onto the stage galloped a company of cowboys. Immediately there was a flashing of rifles and a din of battle. First it seemed as if the heroic rescuers would surely be slaughtered. But they fought bravely and soon the Indians were either killed or captured. Amid the confusion the owners of the prairie schooners leaped to the seats of their wagons, lashed forward their tired horses, and disappeared in safety with the terrified women and children.

It was not until the curtain fell upon this thrilling adventure that Stephen sank back into his chair and drew a long breath.

"Some show, eh, son?" said Mr. Tolman, as they put on their overcoats to leave the theater after the three long acts were over.

The boy looked up, his eyes wide with excitement.

"I should say!" he managed to gasp.

"Did you like it, sonny?" Mr. Ackerman inquired.

"You bet I did!"

"Think you would have preferred to cross the continent by wagon rather than by train?"

Steve hesitated.

"I guess a train would have been good enough for me," he replied. "Was it really as bad as that before the railroads were built?"

"Quite as bad, I'm afraid," was his father's answer. "Sometimes it was even worse, for the unfortunate settlers did not always contrive to escape. It took courage to be a pioneer and travel the country in those days. Undoubtedly there was much romance in the adventure but hand in hand with it went no little peril and discomfort. We owe a great deal to the men who settled the West; and, I sometimes think, even more to the dauntless women."

Stephen did not reply. Very quietly he walked down the aisle between his father and Mr. Ackerman, and when he gave his hand to the latter and said good-night he was still thoughtful. It was evident that the scenes he had witnessed had made a profound impression on him and that he was still immersed in the atmosphere of prairie schooners, lurking Indians, and desert hold-ups. Even when he reached the hotel he was too tense and broad awake to go to bed.

"I wish you'd tell me, Dad, how the first railroad across the country was built," he said. "I don't see how any track was ever laid through such a wilderness. Didn't the Indians attack the workmen? I should think they would have."

His father placed a hand kindly on his shoulder.

"To-morrow we'll talk trans-continental railroads, son, if by that time you still wish to," said he. "But to-night we'll go to bed and think no more about them. I am tired and am sure you must be."

"I'm not!" was the prompt retort.

"I rather fancy you will discover you are after you have undressed," smiled his father. "At any rate we'll have to call off railroading for to-night, for if you are not sleepy, I am."

"But you won't have time to tell me anything to-morrow," grumbled Steve, rising unwillingly from his chair. "You will be busy and forget all about it and—"

"I have nothing to do until eleven o'clock," interrupted Mr. Tolman, "when I have a business meeting to attend. Up to that time I shall be free. And as for forgetting it—well, you might possibly remind me if the promise passes out of my mind."

In spite of himself the boy grinned.

"You can bank on my reminding you all right!" he said, yawning.

"Very well. Then it is a bargain. You do the reminding and I will do the story-telling. Are you satisfied and ready to go to bed and to sleep now?"

"I guess so, yes."

"Good-night then."

"Good-night, Dad. I—I've had a bully day."

CHAPTER XI

THE CROSSING OF THE COUNTRY

In spite of the many excitements crowded into his first day in New York Stephen found that when his head actually touched the pillow sleep was not long in coming and he awoke the next morning refreshed by a heavy and dreamless slumber. He was even dressed and ready for breakfast before his father and a-tiptoe to attack whatever program the day might present.

Fortunately Mr. Tolman was of a sufficiently sympathetic nature to remember how he had felt when a boy, and with generous appreciation for the lad's impatience he scrambled up and made himself ready for a breakfast that was earlier, perhaps, than he would have preferred.

"Well, son," said he, as they took their places in the large dining room, "what is the prospect for to-day? Are you feeling fit for more adventures?"

"I'm primed for whatever comes," smiled the boy.

"That's the proper spirit! Indians, bandits and cowboys did not haunt your pillow then."

"I didn't stay awake to see."

"You are a model traveler! Now we must plan something pleasant for you to do to-day. I am not sure that we can keep up the pace yesterday set us, for it was a pretty thrilling one. Robberies and arrests do not come every day, to say nothing of flotillas of ships and Wild West shows. However, we will do the best we can not to let the day go stale by contrast. But first I must dictate a few letters and glance over the morning paper. This won't take me long and while I am doing it I would suggest that you go into the writing room and send a letter to your mother. I will join you there in half an hour and we will do whatever you like before I go to my meeting. How is that?"

"Righto!"

Accordingly, after breakfast was finished, Steve wandered off by himself in search of paper and ink, and so sumptuous did he find the writing appointments that he not only dashed off a letter to his mother recounting some of the happenings of the previous day, but on discovering a rack of post cards he mailed to Jack Curtis, Tim Barclay, Bud Taylor and some of the other boys patronizing messages informing them that New York was "great" and he was *sorry they were not there*. In fact, it seemed at the moment that all those unfortunate persons who could not visit this magic city were to be profoundly pitied.

In the purchase of stamps for these egoistic missives the remainder of the time passed, and before he realized the half-hour was gone, he saw his father standing in the doorway.

"I am going up to the room now to hunt up some cigars, Steve," announced the elder man. "Do you want to come along or stay here?"

"I'll come with you, Dad," was the quick reply.

The elevator shot them to the ninth floor in no time and soon they were in their room looking down on the turmoil in the street below.

"Some city, isn't it?" commented Mr. Tolman, turning away from the busy scene to rummage through his suit case.

"It's a corker!"

"I thought you would like to go out to the Zoo this morning while I am busy. What do you say?"

"That would be bully."

"It is a simple trip which you can easily make alone. If you like, you can start along now," Mr. Tolman suggested.

"But you said last night that if I would hurry to bed, to-day you would tell me about the Western railroads," objected Stephen.

He saw his father's eyes twinkle.

"You have a remarkable memory," replied he. "I recall now that I did say something of the sort. But surely you do not mean that you would prefer to remain here and talk railroads than to go to the Zoo."

"I can go to the Zoo after you have gone out," maintained Steve, standing his ground valiantly.

"You are a merciless young beggar," grinned his father. "I plainly see that like Shylock you are determined to have your pound of flesh. Well, sit down. We will talk while I smoke."

As the boy settled contentedly into one of the comfortable chintz-covered chairs, Mr. Tolman blew a series of delicate rings of smoke toward the ceiling and wrinkled his brow thoughtfully.

"You got a pretty good idea at the theater last night what America was before we had trans-continental railroads," began he slowly. "You know enough of geography too, I hope, to imagine to some extent what it must have meant to hew a path across such an immense country as ours; lay a roadbed with its wooden ties; and transport all this material as well as the heavy rails necessary for the project. We all think we can picture to ourselves the enormity of the undertaking; but actually we have almost no conception of the difficulties such a mammoth work represented."

He paused, half closing his eyes amid the cloud of smoke.

"To begin with, the promoters of the enterprise received scant encouragement to attack the problem, for few persons of that day had much faith in the undertaking. In place of help, ridicule cropped up from many sources. It was absurd, the public said, to expect such a wild-cat scheme to succeed. Why, over six hundred miles of the area to be covered did not contain a tree and in consequence there would be nothing from which to make cross-ties. And where was the workmen's food to come from if they were plunged into a wilderness beyond the reach of civilization? The thing couldn't be done. It was impossible. Of course it was a wonderful idea. But it never could be carried out. Where were the men to be found who would be willing to take their lives in their hands and set forth to work where Indians or wild beasts were liable to devour them at any moment? Moreover, to build a railroad of such length would take a lifetime and where was the money coming from? For you must remember that the men of that period had no such vast fortunes as many of them have now, and it was no easy task to finance a scheme where the outlay was so tremendous and the probability of success so shadowy. Even as late as 1856 the whole notion was considered visionary by the greater part of the populace."

"But the fun of doing it, Dad!" ejaculated Stephen, with sparkling eyes.

"The fun of it!" repeated his father with a shrug. "Yes, there was fun in the adventure, there is no denying that; and fortunately for the dreamers who saw the vision, men were found who felt precisely as you do. Youth always puts romance above danger, and had there not been these romance lovers it would have gone hard with the trans-continental railroads. We might never have had them. As it was, even the men who ventured to cast in their lot with the promoters had the caution to demand their pay in advance. They had no mind to be deluded into working for a precarious wage. At length enough toilers from the east and from the west were found who were willing to take a chance with their physical safety, and the enterprise was begun."

Stephen straightened up in his chair.

"Had the only obstacle confronting them been the reach of uncharted country ahead that would have been discouraging enough. Fancy pushing your way through eight hundred miles of territory that had never been touched by civilization! And while you are imagining that, do not forget that the slender ribbon of track left behind was your only link with home; and your only hope of getting food, materials, and sometimes water. Ah, you would have had excitement enough to satisfy you had you been one of that company of workmen! On improvised trucks they put up bunks and here they took turns in sleeping while some of their party stood guard to warn them of night raids from Indians and wild beasts. Even in the daytime outposts had to be stationed; and more than once, in spite of every precaution, savages descended on the little groups of builders, overpowered them, and slaughtered many of the number or carried away their provisions and left them to starve. Sometimes marauders tore up the tracks, thereby breaking the connection with the camps in the rear from which aid could be summoned; and in early railroad literature we find many a tale of heroic engineers who ran their locomotives back through almost certain destruction in order to procure help for their comrades. Supply trains were held up and swept clean of their stores; paymasters were robbed, and sometimes murdered, so no money reached the employees; every sort of calamity befell the men. Hundreds of the ten thousand Chinese imported to work at a microscopic wage died of sickness or exposure to the extreme heat or cold."

"Gee!" gasped Stephen, "I'd no idea it was so bad as all that!"

"Most persons have but a faint conception of the price paid for our railways—paid not alone in money but in human life," answered Mr. Tolman. "The route of the western railroads, you see, did not lie solely through flat, thickly wooded country. Our great land, you must remember, is made up of a variety of natural formations, and in crossing from the Atlantic coast to that of the Pacific we get them one after another. In contrast to the forests of mighty trees, with their tangled undergrowth, there were stretches of prairie where no hills broke the level ground; another region contained miles and miles of alkali desert, dry and scorching, where the sun blazed so fiercely down on the steel rails that they became too hot to touch. Here men died of sunstroke and of fever; and some died for want of water. Then directly in the railroad's path arose the towering peaks of the Sierras and Rockies whose snowy crests must be crossed, and whose cold, storms and gales must be endured. Battling with these hardships the workmen were forced to drill holes in the rocky summits and bolt their rough huts down to the earth to prevent them from being blown away."

"I don't see how the thing could have been done!" Steve exclaimed, with growing wonder.

"And you must not forget to add to the chapter of tribulations the rivers that barred the way; the ravines that must either be filled in or bridged; the rocks that had to be blasted out; and the mountains that must be climbed or tunneled."

"I don't see how they ever turned the trick!" the boy repeated.

"It is the same old tale of progress," mused his father. "Over and over again, since time began, men have given their lives that the world might move forward and you and I enjoy the benefits of civilization. Remember it and be grateful to the past and to that vast army of toilers who offered up their all that you might, without effort, profit by the things it took their blood to procure. There is scarcely a comfort you have about you that has not cost myriad men labor, weariness, and perhaps life itself. Therefore value highly your heritage and treat the fruits of all hard work with respect; and whenever you can fit your own small stone into the structure, or advance any good thing that shall smooth the path of those who are to follow you, do it as your sacred duty to those who have so unselfishly builded for you."

There was a moment of silence and the rumble of the busy street rose to their ears.

"I never shall build anything that will help the men of the future," observed Stephen, in a low tone.

"Every human being is building all the time," replied his father. "He is building a strong body that shall mean a better race; a clean mind that shall mean a purer race; a loyalty to country that will result in finer citizenship; and a life of service to his fellows that will bring in time a broader Christianity. Will not the world be the better for all these things? It lies with us to carry forward the good and lessen the evil of the universe, or tear down the splendid ideals for which our fathers struggled and retard the upward march of the universe. If everybody put his shoulder to the wheel and helped the forward spin of our old world, how quickly it would become a better place!"

As he concluded his remarks Mr. Tolman took out his watch.

"Well, well!" said he. "I had no idea it was so late. I must hurry or I shall not finish my story."

"As I told you the men from the east and those from the west worked toward each other from opposite ends of the country. As soon as short lengths of track were finished they were joined together. Near the great Salt Lake of Utah a tie of polished laurel wood banded with silver marked the successful crossing of Utah's territory. Five years later Nevada contributed some large silver spikes to join her length of track to the rest. California sent spikes of solid gold, symbolic both of her cooperation and her mineral wealth; Arizona one of gold, one of silver, and one of iron. Many other States offered significant tributes of similar nature. And when at last the great day came when all the short lines were connected in one whole, what a celebration there was from sea to sea! Wires had been laid so that the hammer that drove the last spike sent the news to cities all over the land. Bells rang, whistles blew, fire alarms sounded. The cost of the Union Pacific was about thirty-nine million dollars and that of the Central Pacific about one hundred and forty million dollars. The construction of the Southern Pacific presented a different set of problems from those of the Northern, but many of the difficulties encountered were the same. Bands of robbers and Indians beset the workmen and either cut the ties and spread the rails, or tore the track up altogether for long distances. Forest fires often overtook the men before they could escape, although trains sometimes contrived to get through the burning areas by drenching their roofs and were able to bring succor to those in peril. Then there were washouts and snowstorms quite as severe as any experienced in the northern country."

"I'm afraid I should have given the whole thing up!" interrupted Steve.

"Many another was of your mind," returned Mr. Tolman. "The frightful heat encountered when crossing the deserts was, as I have said, the greatest handicap. Frequently the work was at a standstill for months because all the metal—rails and tools—became too hot to handle. The difficulty of getting water to the men in order to keep them alive in this arid waste was in itself colossal. Tank cars were sent forward constantly on all the railroads, northern as well as southern, and the suffering experienced when such cars were for various reasons stalled was tremendous. The sand storms along the Southern Pacific route were yet another menace. So you see an eagerness for adventure had to be balanced by a corresponding measure of bravery. Those early days of railroad building were not all romance and picturesqueness."

Stephen nodded as his father rose and took up his hat and coat.

"I'd like to hear Mr. Ackerman tell of the early steamboating," remarked the lad. "I'll bet the story couldn't match the one you have just told."

"Perhaps not," his father replied. "Nevertheless the steamships had their full share of exciting history and you must not be positive in your opinion until you have heard both tales. Now come along, son, if you are going with me, for I must be off."

Obediently Stephen slipped into his ulster and tagged at his father's heels along the corridor.

What a magic country he lived in! And how had it happened that it had been his luck to be born now rather than in the pioneer days when there were not only no railroads but no great hotels like this one, and no elevators?

"I suppose," observed Mr. Tolman, as they went along, "we can hardly estimate what the coming of these railroads meant to the country. All the isolated sections were now blended into one vast territory which brought the dwellers of each into a common brotherhood. It was no small matter to make a unit of a great republic like ours. The seafarer and the woodsman; easterner, westerner, northerner, and southerner exchanged visits and became more intelligently sympathetic. Rural districts were opened up and made possible for habitation. The products of the seacoast and the interior were interchanged. Crops could now be transported; material for clothing distributed; and coal, steel, and iron—on which our industries were dependent—carried wherever they were needed. Commerce took a leap forward and with it national prosperity. From now on we were no longer hampered in our inventions or industries and forced to send to England for machinery. We could make our own engines, manufacture our own rails, coal our own boilers. Distance was diminished until it was no longer a barrier. Letters that it previously took days and even weeks to get came in hours, and the cost and time for freight transportation was revolutionized. In 1804, for example, it took four days to get a letter from New York to Boston; and even as late as 1817 it cost a hundred dollars to move a ton of freight from Buffalo to New York and took twenty days to do it. In every direction the railroads made for national advancement and a more solid United States. No soldiers, no statesmen of our land deserve greater honor as useful citizens than do these men who braved every danger to build across the country our trans-continental railways."

CHAPTER XII

NEW PROBLEMS

have been thinking, Dad," said Steve that evening, while they sat at dinner, "of the railroad story you told me this morning. It was some yarn." His father laughed over the top of his coffee cup.

"It was, wasn't it?" replied he. "And the half was not told then. I was in too much of a hurry to give you an idea of all the trials the poor railroad builders encountered. Did it occur to you, for example, that after the roads to the Pacific coast were laid their managers were confronted by another great difficulty,—the difference in time between the east and the west?"

"I never thought of that," was Steve's answer. "Of course the time must have differed a lot."

"Indeed it did! Every little branch road followed the time peculiar to its own section of the country, and the task of unifying this so that a basis for a common time-table could be adopted was tremendous. A convention of scientists from every section of the country was called to see what could be done about the fifty-three different times in use by the various railroads."

"Fifty-three!" ejaculated Stephen, with a grin. "Why, that was almost as many as Heinz pickles."

"In this case the results of the fifty-three varieties were far more menacing, I am afraid, than those of the fifty-seven," said his father, with a smile, "for travel under such a régime was positively unsafe."

"I can see that it would be. What did they do?"

"Well, after every sort of suggestion had been presented it was decided to divide the country up into four immense parts, separated from one another by imaginary lines running north and south."

"Degrees of longitude?"

"Precisely!" returned Mr. Tolman, gratified that the boy had caught the point so intelligently. "The time of each of these sections jumped fifteen degrees, or one hour, and the railroads lying in each district were obliged to conform to the standard time of their locality. Until this movement went into effect there had been, for example, six so-called standard times to reckon with in going from Boston to Washington."

"I don't see why everybody didn't get smashed up!"

"I don't either; and I fancy the passengers and the railroad people didn't," declared Mr. Tolman. "But with the new state of things the snarl was successfully untangled and the roads began to be operated on a more scientific basis. Then followed gradual improvements in cars which as time went on were made more comfortable and convenient. The invention of the steam engine and the development of our steel products were the two great factors that made our American railroads possible. With the trans-continental roads to carry materials and the opening up of our coal, iron and copper mines we were at last in a position to make our railroads successful. Then science began to evolve wonderful labor-saving machinery which did away with the slow, primitive methods our pioneer engineers had been obliged to employ. The steam shovel was invented, the traveling crane, the gigantic derrick, the pile driver. The early railroad builders had few if any of these devices and were forced to do by hand the work that machinery could have performed in much less time. When one thinks back it is pathetic to consider the number of lives that were sacrificed which under present-day conditions might have been saved. Yet every great movement goes forward over the dead bodies of unnamed heroes. To an extent this is unavoidable and one of the enigmas of life. If every generation were as wise at the beginning as it is at the end there would be no progress. Nevertheless, when you reflect that ten thousand Chinese and Chilean laborers died while building one of the South American railroads it does make us wonder why we should be the ones to reap the benefits of so much that others sowed, doesn't it?" mused the boy's father.

"Do you mean to say that ten thousand persons were killed while that railroad was being built?" questioned Stephen, aghast.

"They were not all killed," was the reply. "Many of them died of exposure to cold, and many from the effects of the climate. Epidemics swept away hundreds of lives. This particular railroad was one of the mightiest engineering feats the world had seen for in its path lay the Andes Mountains, and there was no escape from either crossing or tunneling them. The great tunnel that pierces them at a height of 15,645 feet above sea level is one of the marvels of science. In various parts of the world there are other such monuments to man's conquest of the opposing forces of nature. Honeycombing the Alps are spiral tunnels that curve round and round like corkscrews inside the mountains, rising slowly to the peaks and making it possible to reach the heights that must be traversed. Among these marvels is the Simplon Tunnel, famous the world over. The road that crosses the Semmering Pass from Trieste to Vienna is another example of what man can do if he must. By means of a series of covered galleries it makes its way through the mountains that stretch like a wall between Italy and Austria. In the early days this territory with its many ravines and almost impassable heights would have been considered too difficult to cross. The railroad over the Brenner Pass between Innsbruck and Botzen penetrates the mountains of the Tyrol by means of twenty-three tunnels."

"I learned about the St. Gothard tunnel in school," Steve interrupted eagerly.

"Yes, that is yet another of the celebrated ones," his father rejoined. "In fact, there are now so many of these miracles of skilful railroading that we have almost ceased to wonder at them. Railroads thread their way up Mt. Washington, Mt. Rigi, and many another dizzy altitude; to say nothing of the cable-cars and funicular roads that take our breath away when they whirl us to the top of some mountain, either in Europe or in our own land. Man has left scarce a corner of our planet inaccessible, until now, not content with scaling the highest peaks by train, he has progressed still another stage and is flying over them. Thus do the marvels of one age become the commonplace happenings of the next. Our ancestors doubtless thought, when they had accomplished the miracles of their generation, that nothing could surpass them. In the same spirit we regard our aeroplanes and submarines with triumphant pride. But probably the time will come when those who follow us will look back on what we have done and laugh at our attempts just as you laughed when I told you of the first railroad."

Stephen was thoughtful for a moment.

"It's a great game—living—isn't it, Dad?"

"It is a great game if you make yourself one of the team and pull on the side of the world's betterment," nodded his father. "Think what such a thing as the railroad has meant to millions and millions of people. Not only has it opened up a country which might have been shut away from civilization for centuries; but it has brought men all over the world closer together and made it possible for those of one land to visit those of another and come into sympathy with them. Japan, China, and India, to say nothing of the peoples of Europe, are almost our neighbors in these days of ships and railroads."

"I suppose we should not have known much about those places, should we," reflected the boy.

"Certainly not so much as we do now," was his father's answer. "Of course, travelers did go to those countries now and then; but to get far into their interior in a palanquin carried by coolies, for example, was a pretty slow business."

"And uncomfortable, too," Stephen decided. "I guess the natives were mighty glad to see the railroads coming."

To the lad's surprise his father shook his head.

"I am afraid they weren't," observed he ruefully. "You recall how even the more civilized and better educated English and French opposed the first railroads? Well, the ignorant orientals, who were a hundred times more superstitious, objected very vehemently. The Chinese in particular feared that the innovation would put to flight the spirits which they believed inhabited the earth, air, and water. Surely, they argued, if these gods were disturbed, disaster to the nation must inevitably follow. It was almost impossible to convince even the more intelligent leaders that the railroad would be a benefit instead of a menace for before the ancient beliefs argument was helpless."

"Well, the railroads were built just the same, weren't they?"

"Yes. Fortunately some of the more enlightened were led to see the wisdom of the enterprise, and they converted the others to their views or else overrode their protests. They were like a lot of children who did not know what was best for them and as such they had to be treated. Nevertheless, you may be quite certain that the pioneer days of railroad building in the East were not pleasant ones. Materials had to be carried for great distances both by water and by land. In 1864, when the first locomotive was taken to Ceylon, it had to be transported on a raft of bamboo and drawn from the landing place to the track by elephants."

"Humph!" chuckled Steve. "It's funny to think of, isn't it?"

"More funny to think of than to do, I guess," asserted his father. "Still it is the battle against obstacles that makes life interesting, and in spite of all the hardships I doubt if those first railroad men would have missed the adventure of it all. Out of their resolution, fearlessness and vision came a wonderful fulfillment, and it must have been some satisfaction to know that they had done their share in bringing it about."

"I suppose that is what Mr. Ackerman meant when he spoke of the history of steamboating," said the boy slowly.

"Yes. He and his family had a hand in that great game and I do not wonder he is proud of it. And speaking of Mr. Ackerman reminds me that he called up this afternoon to ask if you would like to take a motor-ride with him to-morrow morning while I am busy."

"You bet I would!" was the fervent reply.

"I thought as much, so I made the engagement for you. He is coming for you at ten o'clock. And he will have quite a surprise for you, too."

"What is it?" the boy asked eagerly.

"It is not my secret to tell," was the provoking answer. "You will know it in good time."

"To-morrow?"

"I think so, yes."

"Can't you tell me anything about it?"

"Nothing but that you were indirectly responsible for it."

"*I!*" gasped Stephen.

Mr. Tolman laughed.

"That will give you something to wonder and to dream about," he responded, rising from the table. "Let us see how much of a Sherlock Holmes you are."

Steve's mind immediately began to speculate rapidly on his father's enigmatic remark. All the way up in the elevator he pondered over the conundrum; and all the evening he turned it over in his mind. At last, tired with the day's activities, he went to bed, hoping that dreams might furnish him with a solution of the riddle. But although he slept hard no dreams came and morning found him no nearer the answer than he had been before.

He must wait patiently for Mr. Ackerman to solve the puzzle.

CHAPTER XIII

DICK MAKES HIS SECOND APPEARANCE

When Mr. Ackerman's car rolled up to the hotel later in the morning the puzzle no longer lacked a solution for in the automobile beside the steamboat magnate sat Dick Martin, the lad of the pocketbook adventure. At first glance Steve scarcely recognized the boy, such a transformation had taken place in his appearance. He wore a new suit of blue serge, a smartly cut reefer, shiny shoes, a fresh cap, and immaculate linen. Soap and water, as well as a proper style of haircut had added their part to the miracle until now, with face glowing and eyes alight with pleasure, Dick was as attractive a boy as one would care to see.

"I have brought Dick along with me, you see," the New Yorker explained, when the three were in the car and speeding up Fifth Avenue. "He and I have been shopping and now he is coming home to stay with me until we hear from one of the schools to which I have written. If they can find a place for him he will start at once. Then he is going to study hard and see what sort of a man he can make of himself. I expect to be very proud of him some day."

The lad flushed.

"I am going to do my best," said he, in a low tone.

"That is all any one can do, sonny," declared Mr. Ackerman kindly. "You'll win out. Don't you worry! I'm not."

He smiled and Dick smiled back timidly.

"Have you been up to Mr. Ackerman's house yet and seen the boats?" Stephen asked, to break the pause that fell between them.

"His collection, you mean? Sure! I'm—staying there."

"Living there, sonny," put in the financier.

"Then I suppose he's told you all about them," went on Stephen, a hint of envy in his tone.

"I haven't yet," laughed their host, "for there hasn't been time. Dick only left the hotel yesterday and we have had a great deal to do since. We had to go to his lodgings and say good-by to the people there who have been kind to him and tell them why he was not coming back. And then there were errands and many other things to see to. So he has not been at home much yet," concluded Mr. Ackerman, with a kindly emphasis on the final sentence.

Dick beamed but it was evident that the magnitude of his good fortune had left him too overwhelmed for words.

Perhaps neither of the boys minded that there was little conversation during the drive for there was plenty to see and to Dick Martin, at least, an automobile ride was such an uncommon experience that it needed no embellishments. They rode up Morningside Drive and back again, looking down on the river as they went, and exclaiming when some unusual craft passed them. Evidently Mr. Ackerman was quite content to let matters take their natural course; but he was not unmindful of his guests and when at last he saw a shadow of fatigue circle Dick's eyes and give place to the glow of excitement that had lighted them he said:

"Now suppose we go back to the house for a while. We have an hour or more before Stephen has to rejoin his father and you two chaps can poke about the suite. What do you say?"

"I WISH YOU'D TELL ME ABOUT THIS QUEER LITTLE OLD-FASHIONED BOAT."

Steve was all enthusiasm. He had been quietly hoping there would be a chance for him to have another peep at the wonderful steamboats.

"I'd like nothing better!" was his instant reply. "I did not see half I wanted to when I was there before, and we go home to-morrow, you know. If I don't see your ships and things to-day I never shall."

"Oh, don't say that!" Mr. Ackerman said quickly. "You and Dick and I are going to be great friends. We are not going to say good-by and never see one another any more. Sometime you will be coming to New York again, I hope. However, if he wants to have a second glimpse of our boats now we'll let him, won't we, Dick?"

Again the boy smiled a timid smile into his benefactor's face.

It did not take long to reach the house and soon the three were in the wonderful room with its panorama of ships moving past the windows and its flotilla of still more ships decorating the walls.

"Now you boys go ahead and entertain yourselves as you please," Mr. Ackerman said. "I am going to sit here and read the paper; but if there is anything you want to ask me you are welcome to do so."

Stephen strolled over to the mantelpiece and stood before the model of the quaint side-wheeler that had held his attention at the time of his first visit; then he stole a furtive glance at the man in the big chair.

"Did you really mean, Mr. Ackerman," he faltered, "that we could ask you questions?"

"Certainly."

"Then I wish you'd tell me about this queer little old-fashioned boat, and how you happened to put it between this up-to-date ocean liner and this battleship."

The elder man looked up.

"That boat that interests you is a model of Fulton's steamboat—or at least as near a model as I could get," explained he. "I put it there to show the progress we have made in shipbuilding since that day."

Steve laughed.

"I see the progress all right," replied he, "but I am afraid I do not know much about Fulton and his side-wheeler."

Mr. Ackerman let the paper slip into his lap.

"I assumed every boy who went to school learned about Robert Fulton," answered he, half teasingly and yet with real surprise.

"I suppose I ought to have learned about him," retorted Stephen, with ingratiating honesty, "and maybe I did once. But if I did I seem to have forgotten about it. You see there are such a lot of those old chaps who did things that I get them all mixed up."

Apparently the sincerity of the confession pleased the capitalist for he laughed.

"I know!" returned he sympathetically. "Every year more and more things roll up to remember, don't they? Had we lived long ago, before so many battles and discoveries had taken place, and so many books been written, life would have been much simpler. Now the learning of all the ages comes piling down on our heads. But at least you can congratulate yourself that you are not so badly off as the boys will be a hundred years hence; they, poor things, will have to learn all about what *we* have been doing, and if the world progresses as rapidly in history and in science as it is doing now, I pity them. Not only will they have to go back to Fulton but to him they will probably have to add a score of other inventors."

Both boys joined in the steamboat man's hearty laugh.

"Well, who was Fulton, anyway, Mr. Ackerman?" Stephen persisted.

"If you want me to tell you that Robert Fulton was the first American to make a successful steamboat I can give you that information in a second," was the reply. "But if you wish to hear how he did it that is a much longer story."

"I like stories," piped Dick from the corner of the couch where he was sitting.

"So do I," echoed Steve.

"Then I see there is no help for me!" Mr. Ackerman answered, taking off his spectacles and putting them into the case.

With an anticipatory smile Stephen seated himself on the great leather divan beside the other boy.

"Before the steamboat came," began Mr. Ackerman, "you must remember that paddle wheels had long been used, for both the Egyptians and the Romans had built galleys with oars that moved by a windlass turned by the hands of slaves or by oxen. Later there were smaller boats whose paddle wheels were driven by horses. So you see paddle wheels were nothing new; the world was just waiting for something that would turn them around. After the Marquis of Worcester had made his steam fountain he suggested that perhaps this power might be used to propel a boat but unfortunately he died before any experiments with the idea could be made. Various scientists, however, in Spain, France, England and Scotland caught up the plan but after struggling unsuccessfully with it for a time abandoned it as impractical. In 1802 Lord Dundas, a proprietor in one of the English canals, made an encouraging start by using a towboat with a paddle wheel at its stern. But alas, this contrivance kicked up such a fuss in the narrow stream that it threatened to tear the banks along the edge all to pieces and therefore it was given up and for ten years afterward there was no more steamboating in England."

The boys on the couch chuckled.

"In the meantime in America thoughtful men were mulling over the problem of steam navigation. Watt's engine had opened to the minds of inventors endless possibilities; and the success of the early railroads made many persons feel that a new era of science, whose wonders had only begun to unfold, was at hand. In Connecticut there lived a watchmaker by the name of John Fitch, who, although he knew little of the use of steam, knew much about machinery. Through the aid of a company that furnished him with the necessary money he built a steamboat which was tried out in 1787 and made three miles an hour. Of course it was not a boat like any of ours for it was propelled by twelve oars, or paddles, operated by a very primitive steam engine. Nevertheless, it was the forerunner of later and better devices of a similar nature, and therefore Fitch is often credited with being the inventor of the steamboat. Perhaps, had he been able to go on with his schemes, he might have given the world something really significant in this direction; but as it was he simply pointed the way. His money gave out, the company would do nothing further for him, and after building a second boat that could go eight miles an hour instead of three he became discouraged and intemperate and let his genius go to ruin, dying later in poverty—a sad end to a life that might well have been a brilliant one. After Fitch came other experimenters, among them Oliver Evans of Philadelphia who seems to have been a man of no end of inventive vision."

"Wasn't he the one who tried sails on a railroad train?" inquired Steve, noting with pleasure the familiar name.

"He was that very person," nodded Mr. Ackerman. "He evidently had plenty of ideas; the only trouble was that they did not work very well. He had already applied steam to mills and wagons, and now he wanted to see what he could do with it aboard a boat. Either he was very impractical or else hard luck pursued his undertakings. At any rate, he had a boat built in Kentucky, an engine installed on it, and then he had the craft floated to New Orleans from which point he planned to make a trip up the Mississippi. But alas, before his boat was fully ready, there was a drop in the river and the vessel was left high and dry on the shore."

"Jove!" exclaimed Dick involuntarily.

"Pretty tough, wasn't it?" remarked Mr. Ackerman.

"What did he do then?" demanded Stephen. "Did he resurrect the boat?"

"No, it did not seem to be any use; instead he had the engine and boiler taken out and put into a saw mill where once again hard luck pursued him, for the mill was burned not long after. That was the end of Oliver Evans's steamboating."

Mr. Ackerman paused thoughtfully.

"Now while Fitch and those following him were working at the steamboat idea here in America, Robert Fulton, also a native of this country, was turning the notion over in his mind. Strangely enough, he had not intended to be an inventor for he was in France, studying to be a painter. During a visit to England he had already met several men who were interested in the steam engine and through them had informed himself pretty thoroughly about the uses and action of steam. In Paris he made the acquaintance of a Mr. Barlow and the two decided to raise funds and build a steamboat to run on the Rhone. This they did, but unfortunately the boat sank before any degree of success had been achieved. Then Fulton, not a whit discouraged, told the French Government that if they would furnish the money he would build a similar boat to navigate the Seine. The French, however, had no faith in the plan and promptly refused to back it."

"I'll bet they wished afterward they had!" interrupted Dick.

"I presume they did," agreed Mr. Ackerman. "It is very easy to see one's mistakes after a thing is all over. Anyway, Mr. Barlow came back to America, where Fulton joined him, and immediately the latter went to building a steamboat that should be practical. On his way home he had stopped in England and purchased various parts for his engine and when he got to New York he had these set up in an American boat. You must not for a moment imagine that everything about this first steamboat of Fulton's was original. On the contrary he combined what was best in the experiments of previous inventors. He adopted the English type of engine, the side paddle, everything that seemed to him workable. Barlow and a rich New Yorker named Livingston backed the enterprise. Now some time before the State of New York, half in jest and half in irony, had granted to Livingston the sole right to navigate the New York waters by means of ships driven by steam or fire engines. At the time the privilege had caused much mirth for there were nothing but sailing ships in existence, and there was no prospect of there ever being any other kind of vessel. Hence the honor was a very empty one and nobody expected a time would arrive when it would ever be of any value to its owner. But Livingston was a shrewder and more far-seeing man than were the old legislators at Albany, and to Fulton he was an indispensable ally."

The boy listened breathlessly.

"How these three men managed to keep their secret so well is a mystery; but apparently they did, and when Fulton suddenly appeared on the Hudson with a steamboat named the *Clermont* for Mr. Livingston's country seat on the Palisades, the public was amazed. A model of the boat with a miniature engine had previously been tried out so the three promoters had little doubt that their project would work, and it did. As the new craft moved along without any sails to propel it the sensation it made was tremendous. People were divided as to whether to flee from it in terror or linger and marvel at it. It is a pity that the newspapers of the period did not take the advent of this remarkable invention more seriously for it would have been interesting to know more of the impression it created. As it was little is recorded about it. Probably the very silence of the press is significant of the fact that there was scant faith in the invention, and that it was considered too visionary a scheme to dignify with any notice. However that may be, the newspapers passed this wonderful event by with almost no comment. History, however, is more generous and several amusing stories have come down to us of the fright the *Clermont* caused as she crept along the river at dusk with a shower of vermilion sparks rising from her funnel. One man who came around a bend of the stream in his boat and encountered the strange apparition for the first time told his wife afterward that he had met the devil traveling the river in a sawmill."

There was a shout of laughter from the boys.

"The trial trip, to which many distinguished guests were invited, took place a few days later, and after improving some of the defects that cropped up the steamboat was advertised to run regularly between New York and Albany. Now if you think this announcement was hailed with joy you are much mistaken," continued Mr. Ackerman, smiling to himself at some memory that evidently amused him. "On the contrary the owners of the sailing ships which up to this time had had the monopoly of traffic were furious with rage. So vehemently did they maintain that the river belonged to them that at last the matter went to the courts and Daniel Webster was retained as Fulton's counsel. The case attracted wide attention throughout the country, and when it was decided in Fulton's favor there was great excitement. Every sort of force was brought to bear to thwart the new steamboat company. Angry opponents tried to blow up the boat as it lay at the dock; attempts were made to burn it. At length affairs became so serious that a clause was appended to the court's decree which made it a public crime punishable by fine or imprisonment to attempt to injure the *Clermont*."

Mr. Ackerman paused to light a fresh cigar.

"From the moment the law took this stand the success of the undertaking became assured and it is interesting to see how quickly the very men who jeered loudest at the enterprise now came fawning and begging to have a part in it. Other steamboats were added to the line and soon rival firms began to construct steamboats of their own and try to break up Fulton's monopoly of the waters of the State. For years costly lawsuits raged, and in defiance of the right the New York legislature had granted to Livingston, the fiercest competition took place. Sometime I should like to tell you more of this phase of the story for it is a very exciting and interesting yarn. Yet in spite of all the strife and hatred that pursued him Fulton's river-boats and ferries continued to run."

"The State stuck to its bargain, then," murmured Steve, "and left Livingston the rights awarded him?"

"No," replied Mr. Ackerman. "For a time they clung to their agreement; but at last the courts withdrew the right as illegal, and poor Livingston, who had sunk the greater part of his fortune in the steamboat business, lived to see the fruit of his toil wrested from him. In point of fact, I believe the decision of the courts to have been a just one for no one person or group of persons should control the waterways of the country. You can see the wisdom of this yourself. Nevertheless, the decree hit Livingston pretty hard. It was the first step in the destruction of a monopoly," added Mr. Ackerman whimsically. "Since then such decrees have become common happenings in America, monopolies being considered a menace to national prosperity. Certainly in this case it was well that the Supreme Court of the United States decided that all waters of the country should be free to navigators, no matter in what kind of vessel they chose to sail."

"It was tough on Fulton and his friends, though, wasn't it?" observed Dick, who was plainly unconvinced as many another had been of the justice of the arguments.

"Yes," agreed Mr. Ackerman, smiling into his troubled eyes, "I grant you it was tough on them."

CHAPTER XIV

A STEAMBOAT TRIP BY RAIL

It was with a sense of deep regret that Stephen bade good-by to Mr. Ackerman and Dick and returned to the hotel to join his father. For the steamboat financier he had established one of those ardent admirations which a boy frequently cherishes toward a man of attractive personality who is older than himself; and for Dick he had a genuine liking. There was a quality very winning in the youthful East-sider and now that the chance for betterment had come his way Steve felt sure that the boy would make good. There was a lot of pluck and grit in that wiry little frame; a lot of honesty too, Stephen reflected, with a blush. He was not at all sure but that in the matter of fearlessness and moral courage the New York lad had the lead of him. Certainly he was not one who shrank from confessing when he had been at fault which, Steve owned with shame, could not be said of himself.

For several days he had not thought of his automobile escapade but now once more it came to his mind, causing a cloud to chase the joyousness from his face. Alas, was he never to be free of the nagging mortification that had followed that single act? Was it always to lurk in the background and make him ashamed to confront the world squarely? Well, it was no use regretting it now. He had made his choice and he must abide by it.

Nevertheless he was not quite so spontaneously happy when he met his father at luncheon and recounted to him the happenings of the morning.

"Mr. Ackerman is taking a big chance with that boy," was Mr. Tolman's comment, when a pause came in the narrative. "I only hope he will not disappoint him. There must be a great difference between the standards of the two. However, Dick has some fine characteristics to build on—honesty and manliness. I think the fact that he showed no coward blood and was ready to stand by what he had done appealed to Ackerman. It proved that although they had not had the same opportunity in life they at least had some good stuff in common. You can't do much with a boy who isn't honest."

Stephen felt the blood beating in his cheeks.

Fortunately his father did not notice his embarrassment and as they soon were on their way to a picture show the memory that had so importunately raised its unwelcome head was banished by the stirring story of a Californian gold mine. Therefore by the time Stephen was ready to go to bed the ghost that haunted him was once more thrust into the background and he had gained his serenity. No, he was not troubled that night by dreams of his folly nor did he awaken with any remembrance of it. Instead he and his father chatted as they packed quite as pleasantly as if no specter stood between them.

"Well, son, have you enjoyed your holiday?" inquired Mr. Tolman, as they settled themselves in the great plush chairs of the parlor car and waited for the train to start.

"Yes, I've had a bully time, Dad."

"I'm glad of that," was the kind reply. "It was unlucky that my business took up so much more of my time than I had expected and that I had to leave you to amuse yourself instead of going about with you, as I had planned. It was too bad. However, if you have managed to get some fun out of your visit that is the main thing. In fact, I am not sure but that you rather enjoyed going about alone," concluded he mischievously.

Stephen smiled but did not reply. There was no denying that he had found being his own master a pleasant experience which had furnished him with a gratifying sense of freedom and belief in his own importance. What a tale he would have to tell the fellows at home! And how shocked his mother would be to hear that he had been turned loose in a great city in this unceremonious fashion! He could hear her now saying to his father:

"I don't see what you were thinking of, Henry, to let Stephen tear about all alone in a city like New York. I should have worried every instant if I had known what he was doing. Suppose anything had happened to him!"

Well, mercifully, nothing had happened,—that is, nothing worse than his falling into the hands of a detective and being almost arrested for robbery, reflected the boy with a grin.

Perhaps Mr. Tolman interpreted his thoughts for presently he observed with a smile:

"It is time you were branching out some for yourself, anyway, son. You are old enough now to be treated like a man, not like a little boy."

As he spoke he looked toward Stephen with an expression of such pride and affection that the force of it swept over the lad as it never had done before. What a bully sort his father was, he suddenly thought; and how genuinely he believed in him! Why not speak out now and clear up the wretched deception he had practiced, and start afresh with a clean conscience? With impulsive resolve he gripped the arms of the chair and pulled himself together for his confession. But just at the crucial moment there was a stir in the aisle and a porter followed by two belated passengers hurried into the train which was on the brink of departure. That they had made their connection by a very narrow margin was evident in their appearance, for both were hot and out of breath, and the stout colored porter puffed under the stress of his haste and the heavy luggage which weighed him down.

"It's these two chairs, sir," he gasped, as he tossed the new leather suit case into the rack. "Is there anything else I can do for you?"

"No," replied the traveler, thrusting a bill into the darkey's hand. Already the train was moving. "Keep the change," he added quickly.

"Thank you, sir! Thank you!" stammered the vanishing negro.

"Well, we caught it, didn't we, Dick? It didn't look at one time as if it were possible. That block of cars on the avenue was terrible. But we are off now! It was about the closest shave I ever made." Then he turned around. "Hullo!" he cried. "Who's this? Bless my soul!"

Both Mr. Tolman and Steve joined in the laugh of amazement.

"Well, if this isn't a great note!" went on Mr. Ackerman, still beaming with surprise. "I thought you people were not going until the afternoon train."

"I managed to finish up my business yesterday and get off earlier than I planned," Mr. Tolman explained. "But I did not know *you* had any intention of going in this direction."

"I hadn't until this morning," laughed the financier. "Then a telegram arrived saying they could take Dick at the New Haven school to which I had written if he entered right away, at the beginning of the term. So I dropped everything and here we are *en route*. It was rather short notice and things were a bit hectic;

but by turning the whole apartment upside down, rushing our packing, and keeping the telephone wire hot we contrived to make the train."

"It is mighty nice for us," put in Mr. Tolman cordially. "So Dick is setting forth on his education, is he?"

"Yes, he is starting out to make of himself a good scholar, a good sport, a good athlete, and I hope a good man," returned the New Yorker.

"A pretty big order, isn't it, Dick?" laughed Mr. Tolman.

"It seems so," returned the boy.

"It is not a bit too big," interrupted Mr. Ackerman. "Dick knows he hasn't got to turn the trick all in a minute. He and I understand such things take time. But they *can be done* and we expect we are going to do them."

He flashed one of his rare smiles toward his protégé and the lad smiled back frankly.

"I expect so, too," echoed Mr. Tolman. "You've got plenty of backers behind you, Dick, and you have a clear path ahead. That is all any boy needs."

"You're going back to school, aren't you, youngster?" Mr. Ackerman suddenly inquired of Stephen.

"Yes, sir. I start in next week."

"Decided yet whether you will be a railroad man like your Dad, or a steamboat man like me?" went on the New Yorker facetiously.

"Not yet."

"Oh, for shame! It should not take you any time at all to decide a question like that," the capitalist asserted teasingly. "What's hindering you?"

Stephen gave a mischievous chuckle.

"I can't decide until I have heard both sides," said he. "So far I know only half the steamboat story."

"I see! In other words you think that between here and New Haven I might beguile the time by going on with the yarn I began yesterday."

"That thought crossed my mind, sir,—yes."

"You should go into the diplomatic service, young man. Your talents are being wasted," observed Mr. Ackerman good-humoredly. "Well, I suppose I could romance for the benefit of you two boys for part of the way, at least. It will give your father, Steve, a chance to go into the other car and smoke. Where did we break off our story? Do you remember?"

"Where the United States said anybody had the right to sail anywhere he wanted to, in any kind of a boat he chose," piped Dick with promptness.

"Yes, yes. I recall it all now," said Mr. Ackerman. "The courts withdrew the grant giving Livingston the sole right to navigate the waters of New York State by means of steamboats. So you want to hear more about it, do you?"

"Yes!" came simultaneously from both the boys.

"Then all aboard! Tolman, you can read, or run off and enjoy your cigar. We are going on a steamboat cruise."

"Push off! You won't bother me," was the tolerant retort, as the elder man unfolded the morning paper.

Mr. Ackerman cleared his throat.

"Before this decree to give everybody an equal chance in navigating the waters of the country was handed down by the courts," he began, "various companies, in defiance of Livingston's contract, began building and running steamboats on the Hudson. Two rival boats were speedily in operation and it was only after a three years' lawsuit that they were legally condemned and handed over to Fulton to be broken up. Then the ferryboat people got busy and petitioned the New York Legislature for the right to run their boats to and fro between the New York and New Jersey sides of the river, and it is interesting to remember that it was on one of these ferry routes that Cornelius Vanderbilt, the great American financier, began his career."

"I never knew that!" ejaculated Dick, intent on the story.

"After the ruling of the Supreme Court in 1818 that all the waters of the country were free there was a rush to construct and launch steamers on the Hudson. The route was, you see, not only the most direct one between Albany and New York but it also lay in the line of travel between the eastern States and those of the west which were just being opened to traffic by the railroads and ships of the Great Lakes. Now you must not for a moment imagine that in those days there were any such vast numbers of persons traversing the country as there are now. Our early Americans worked hard and possessed only comparatively small fortunes so they had little money to throw away on travel simply for its own sake; moreover the War of 1812 had left the country poor. Nevertheless there were a good many persons who were obliged to travel, and it followed that each of the Hudson River lines of steamers was eager to secure their patronage. Hence a bitter competition arose between the rival steamboat companies."

He paused and smiled whimsically at some memory that amused him.

"Every inducement was offered the public by these battling forces. The older vessels were scrapped or reduced to tug service and finer steamboats were built; and once upon the water the engines were driven at full speed that quicker trips might lure passengers to patronize the swifter boats. Captains and firemen pitted their energies against one another and without scruple raced their ships, with the result that there were many accidents. In spite of this, however, the rivalry grew rather than diminished."

"It must have been great sport," remarked Stephen.

"Oh, there was sport in plenty," nodded Mr. Ackerman. "Had you lived during those first days of Hudson River transportation you would have seen all the sport you wanted to see, for the steamboat feud raged with fury, the several companies trying their uttermost to get the trade away from the Fulton people and from one another. Money became no object, the only aim being to win in the game. Fares were reduced from ten dollars to one, and frequently passengers were carried for nothing simply for the sheer spite of getting them away from other lines. Vanderbilt was in the thick of the fray, having now accumulated sufficient fortune to operate no less than fifty boats. Among the finest vessels were those of the Emerald Line; and the *Swallow* and the *Rochester,* two of the speediest rivals, were continually racing each other. The devices resorted to in order to ensnare passengers were very amusing: some boats carried bands; others served free meals; and because there were few newspapers in those days, and only limited means for advertising, runners were hired to go about the city or waylay prospective travelers at the docks and try to coax them into making their trip by some particular steamer."

"That was one way of getting business!" laughed Steve.

"And often a very effective way, too," rejoined Mr. Ackerman. "In June of 1847 a tremendously exciting race took place between the *Oregon* and the *Vanderbilt,* then a new boat, for a thousand dollars a side. The steamers left the Battery at eleven o'clock in the morning and a dense crowd turned out to see them start. For thirty miles they kept abreast; then the *Oregon* gained half a length and in passing the other boat bumped into her, damaging her wheelhouse. It was said at the time that the disaster was not wholly an accident. Certainly there were grounds for suspicion. As you may imagine, the calamity roused the rage of the competing boat. But the commander of the *Oregon* was undaunted by what he had done. All he wished was to win the race and that he was determined to do. He got up a higher and higher pressure of steam, and used more and more coal until, when it was time to return to New York, he discovered that his supply had given out and that he had no more fuel."

"And he had to give up the race?" queried Dick breathlessly.

"Not he! He wasn't the giving-up kind," said Mr. Ackerman. "Finding nothing at hand to run his boilers with he ordered all the expensive fittings of the boat to be torn up and cast into the fire—woodwork, furniture, carvings; anything that would burn. In that way he kept up his furious rate of speed and came in victorious by the rather close margin of twelve hundred feet."

"Bully for him!" cried Dick.

But Stephen did not echo the applause.

"It was not a square race," he said, "and he had no right to win. Anyway, his steamboat must have been pretty well ruined."

"I fancy it was an expensive triumph," owned Mr. Ackerman. "Without doubt it cost much more than the thousand dollars he won to repair the vessel. Still, he had the glory, and perhaps it was worth it to the company."

"Were there other races like that?" Dick asked.

"Yes, for years the racing went on until there were so many fires, explosions and collisions, that the steamer inspection law was put through to regulate the conditions of travel. It certainly was high time that something was done to protect the public, too, for such universal recklessness prevailed that everybody was in danger. Boats were overloaded; safety valves were plugged;

boilers carried several times as much steam as they had any right to do, and many lives had been sacrificed before the government stepped in and put a stop to this strife for fame and money. Since then the traffic on the Hudson has dropped to a plane of sanity and is now carried on by fine lines of boats that conform to the rules for safety and efficient service."

"And what became of Mr. Vanderbilt?" interrogated Dick, who was a New Yorker to the core and had no mind to lose sight of the name with which he was familiar.

"Oh, Mr. Vanderbilt was a man who had many irons in the fire," replied Mr. Ackerman, smiling at the boy's eagerness. "He did not need to be pitied for just about this time gold was discovered in California and as the interest of the country swung in that direction Vanderbilt, ever quick to seize an opening wherever it presented itself, withdrew some of his steamers from the Hudson and headed them around to the Pacific coast instead."

"And your family, Mr. Ackerman, were mixed up in all this steamboat rumpus?" commented Steve suddenly.

"Yes, my grandfather was one of the Hudson River racers and quite as bad as the rest of them," the man replied. "Nevertheless he was a stanch, clever old fellow, and because he did his part toward building up the commerce and prosperity of the nation I have always regarded him with the warmest respect. I do not approve of all his methods, however, any more than I approve of many of the cut-throat business methods of to-day which sometime will be looked back upon with as much shame as these have been. There are moments, I must confess, when I wonder if we, with all our supposed enlightenment, have made any very appreciable advance over the frank and open racing done by our forefathers on the Hudson," reflected he half-humorously. "Perhaps we are a trifle more humane; and yet there is certainly much to be desired in the way we still sacrifice the public to our greed for money. An evil sometimes has to come to a climax to make us conscious of our injustice. Let us hope that our generation will not be so blind that it will not heed the warnings of its conscience, and instead delay until some such catastrophe comes upon it as pursued the racing boats of the Hudson River."

CHAPTER XV

THE ROMANCE OF THE CLIPPER SHIP

It was with genuine regret that Mr. Tolman and Stephen parted from Mr. Ackerman and Dick when the train reached New Haven.

"We shall not say good-by to Dick," Mr. Tolman declared, "for he is not to be very far away and I hope sometime he will come to Coventry and spend a holiday with us. Why don't you plan to do that too, Ackerman? Run over from New York for Thanksgiving and bring the boy with you. Why not?"

"That is very kind of you."

"But I mean it," persisted Mr. Tolman. "It is no perfunctory invitation. Plan to do it. We should all be delighted to have you. There is nothing in the world Mrs. Tolman loves better than a houseful of guests. Doris will be home from college and I should like you to see what a fine big daughter I have. As for Steve—"

"I wish you would come, Mr. Ackerman," interrupted the boy.

Mr. Ackerman hesitated.

"I tell you what we'll do," replied he at length. "We'll leave it to Dick. If he makes a good record at school and earns the holiday we will accept your invitation. If he doesn't we won't come. Is that a bargain, youngster?" he concluded, turning to the lad at his side.

The boy flushed.

"It is a rather stiff one, sir," he answered, with a laughing glance.

"I think that's playing for too high stakes, Ackerman," Mr. Tolman objected. "It is a little rough to put all the burden on Dick. Suppose we divide up the responsibility and foist half of it on Stephen? Let us say you will come if both boys make good in their studies and conduct."

Dick drew a breath of relief at the words, regarding the speaker with gratitude.

"That is a squarer deal, isn't it?" continued Mr. Tolman.

"I think so—yes," was Dick's response.

"And you, Steve—do you subscribe to the contract?"

"Yes, I'll sign," grinned Stephen.

"Then the agreement is clinched," exclaimed his father, "and it will be the fault of you two young persons if we do not have a jolly reunion at Thanksgiving time. Good-by Ackerman! Good-by, Dick. Good luck to you! We are pinning our faith on you, remember. Don't disappoint us."

"I'll try not to," the boy answered, as he stepped to the platform.

"Dick is a fine, manly young chap," observed Mr. Tolman, after the train was once more under way and he and Stephen were alone. "I have a feeling that he is going to make good, too. All he needed was a chance. He has splendid stuff in him. There isn't a mean bone in his body."

Stephen moved uncomfortably in his chair and a guilty blush rose to his cheek but apparently his father did not notice it.

"You liked Mr. Ackerman also, didn't you, son? Indeed there is no need to ask for he is a genius with young people and no boy could help liking a man of his type. It is a pity he hasn't a dozen children, or isn't the leader of a boy's school."

"He is corking at story-telling!" was Steve's comment.

"He certainly is. I caught some fragments of his Hudson River tale and did not wonder that it fascinated you. What a remarkable era that was!" he mused.

"There were a lot of questions I wanted to ask him," Stephen said.

"Such as?"

"Well, for one thing I was curious to know what happened after the steamers on the Hudson were proved a success."

"I can answer that question," replied his father promptly. "After the river boats had demonstrated their practicability steamships were built for traffic along short distances of the coast. Owing to the War of 1812 and the danger to our shipping from the British, however, the launching of these new lines did not take place immediately; but in time the routes were established. The first of these was from New York to New Haven. You see, travel by steam power was still so much of a novelty that Norwich, first proposed as a destination, was felt to be too far away. It was like taking one's life in one's hands to venture such an immense distance from land on a steamboat."

Stephen smiled with amusement.

"But gradually," continued Mr. Tolman, "the public as well as the steamboat companies became more daring and a line from New York to Providence, with Vanderbilt's *Lexington* as one of the ships, was put into operation. Then in 1818 a line of steamers to sail the Great Lakes was built; and afterwards steamships to travel to points along the Maine coast. The problem of navigation on the rivers of the interior of the country followed and here a new conundrum in steamboat construction confronted the builders, for the channels of many of the streams were shallow and in consequence demanded a type of boat very long and wide in proportion to its depth of hull. After such a variety of boat had been worked out and constructed, lines were established on several of the large rivers, and immediately the same old spirit of rivalry that pervaded the Hudson years before cropped up in these other localities. Bitter competition, for example, raged between the boats that plied up and down the Mississippi; and in 1870 a very celebrated race took place between the *Natchez* and the *Robert E. Lee.* The distance to be covered was 1218 miles and the latter ship made it in three days, eighteen hours, and thirty minutes. The test, however, was not a totally fair one since the *Natchez* ran into a fog that held her up for six hours. But the event illustrates the keen interest with which men followed the progress of American shipping; and you can see how natural it was that after the river boats, lake steamers, coastwise vessels and tugs had had their day the next logical step (and very prodigious one) was the—"

"The ocean liner!" ejaculated Stephen.

"Precisely!" nodded his father. "Now there are two separate romances of our ocean-going ships. The first one is of the sailing vessels and is a chronicle of adventure and bravery as enthralling as any you could wish to read. I wish I had time to tell it to you in full and do it justice, but I fear I can only sketch in a few of the facts and leave you to read the rest by yourself some time. You probably know already that whalers went out from Gloucester, New Bedford, and various of our eastern ports and often were gone on two or three-year cruises; and when you recall that in those early days there not only was no wireless but not even the charts, lighthouses, and signals of a thoroughly surveyed coast you will appreciate that setting forth on such a voyage for whale-oil (then used almost exclusively for lighting purposes) took courage. Of course the captains of the ships had compasses for the compass came into use just before the beginning of the Fifteenth Century and was one of the things that stimulated the Portuguese and Spaniards to start out on voyages of discovery. The Spaniards built ships that were then considered the largest and finest afloat, and probably Columbus caught the enthusiasm of the period and with the newly invented compass to guide him was stirred to brave the ocean and discover other territory to add to the riches of the land he loved. It was a golden age of romance and adventure and the journeys of Columbus grew out of it quite naturally. But in America shipping had its foundation in no such picturesque beginning. The first vessel made in this country was constructed as a mere matter of necessity, being built at the mouth of the Kennebec River to carry back to England a group of disheartened, homesick settlers."

He paused thoughtfully a moment.

"Even the ships of later date had their birth in the same motive—that of necessity. The early colonists were forced to procure supplies from England and they had no choice but to build ships for that purpose. At first these sailing packets were very small, and as one thinks of them to-day it is to marvel that they ever made so many trips without foundering. As for our coastwise ships, up to 1812 they were nothing more than schooner-rigged hulls."

"I wonder where the word *schooner* came from," commented Steve.

"The legend goes that the term *scoon* was a colloquialism used when skipping stones. When a pebble glanced along the top of the water it was said to *scoon*," answered his father, with a smile. "After the War of 1812 was over and our American vessels were safe from possible attack, and after the country itself had recovered somewhat from the stress of this financial burden so that men had more money to invest in commerce, we began to branch out and build finer vessels; and when it came to rigging them there seemed to be no name to apply to the arrangement of the sails. The story goes that one day as one of these new ships sailed out of Gloucester harbor a fisherman watching her exclaimed with admiration, 'See her *scoon!*' The phrase not only caught the public fancy but that of the shipbuilders as well, and the word *schooner* was quickly adopted."

"I never knew that before!" announced Steve, when the narrative was concluded.

"Slowly the models of ships improved," went on his father, without heeding the interruption. "Vessels became larger, faster, more graceful. Even the whalers and fishing smacks took on more delicate lines. Merchants from Salem, Gloucester, New Bedford invested their hard-earned savings in whalers and trading ships, and many of them made their fortunes by so doing. The sailing packets that went to Liverpool began to make excellent time records. Although the English were now using steamers for trans-Atlantic travel they had not perfected them to a sufficient extent to make their trips faster than those of sailing ships."

"About how long did it take them to cross?" inquired Stephen.

"The average time to Liverpool was from nineteen to twenty-one days," was the answer. "And for the return voyage from thirty to thirty-five."

"Whew, Dad! Why, one could walk it in that time!" exclaimed the lad.

"It was a long time," his father agreed. "But it is not fair to measure it by present-day standards. Think how novel a thing it was to cross the ocean at all!"

"I suppose so," came reflectively from Stephen.

"It was not long," continued his father, "before the English improved their engines so that their steamers made better time, and then our American sailing packets were left far behind. This, as you can imagine, did not please our proud and ambitious colonists who were anxious to increase their commerce and build up their young and growing country. Something must be done! As yet they had not mastered the enigma of steam but they could make their sailing ships swifter and finer and this they set to work to do. Out of this impetus for prosperity came the remarkable clipper-ship era.

"We shall probably never see such beautiful ships again," continued Mr. Tolman, a trifle sadly. "Youth and romance go hand in hand, and our country was very young, and proud and eager in those days. Our commerce was only beginning and the far corners of the world were strange, unexplored and alluring. It is like an Arabian Night's Tale to read of those wonderful ships built to carry merchandise to China, India and other foreign ports. Speed was their aim—speed, speed, speed! They must hold their own against the English steamers if they would keep their place on the seas. For in those days the methods of packing produce were very primitive, and it was imperative that such perishable things as tea, dried fruits, spices and coffee should be rushed to the markets before the dampness spoiled them. If they mildewed they would be a dead loss to the merchants handling them. Moreover as cable and telegraph were unknown there was no way to keep in touch with the demands of the public, or be sure of prices. Therefore every merchant hurried his goods home in the hope of being the first in the field and reaping the largest profits."

"More racing!" exclaimed Stephen.

"It was racing, indeed!" returned his father. "Ships raced one another back from China, each trying desperately to discharge her cargo before her rival did. Like great sea-birds these beautiful boats skimmed the waves, stretching every inch of canvas to be the winner at the goal. As a result the slow merchant packets with their stale cargoes could find no patrons, the clippers commanding not only all the trade but the highest prices for produce as well. Silks, chinaware, ivory, bamboo—all the wealth of the Orient began to arrive in America where it was hungrily bought up, many a man making his fortune in the East India trade. Of this fascinating epoch Hawthorne gives us a vivid picture."

"It must have been great to travel on one of those ships!" said Stephen.

"It was not all pleasure, by any means, son," Mr. Tolman replied. "Often the vessels encountered hurricanes and typhoons in the treacherous Eastern waters. Sometimes ships were blown out of their course and wrecked, or cast ashore on islands where their crews became the prey of cannibals."

"Jove!"

"It had its outs—this cruising to distant ports," announced his father. "Moreover, the charts in use were still imperfect and lighthouse protection was either very scanty or was lacking entirely."

"What became of the clipper ships?"

"Well, we Americans never do anything by halves, you know. When we go in we go in all over," laughed his father. "That is what we did with our clipper ships. We were so pleased with them that we built more and more, sending them everywhere we could think of. Many went around to California to carry merchandise to the gold searchers. At last there were so many of these swift vessels that they cut into one another and freight rates dropped. Besides, steamboats were coming into general use and were now running on all the more important ocean routes. The day of the sailing ship was over and the marvelous vessels were compelled to yield their place to the heralds of progress and become things of the past. Nevertheless, their part in our American commerce will never be forgotten and we have them to thank not only for the fame they brought our country but also for much of its wealth."

With a quick gesture of surprise he rose hurriedly.

"See!" he exclaimed. "We are almost home. We have talked 'ships and sealing-wax' for hours."

"It hasn't seemed for hours," retorted Stephen, springing to collect his luggage.

"Nor to me, either."

"Some time I'd like to hear about the ocean liners," ventured the boy.

"You must get Mr. Ackerman to tell you that story when he comes to visit us Thanksgiving," was the reply, "if he *does* come. That part of it seems to be up to you and Dick."

"I mean to do my part to get him here," Steve announced. "I hope Dick will plug, too."

"I rather think you can trust him for that," was the quiet answer.

CHAPTER XVI

AGAIN THE MAGIC DOOR OPENS

A change of trains and a brief hour's journey brought the travelers safely to Coventry where Havens met them with the automobile.

"This will be our last ride this fall," observed Mr. Tolman, as he loitered on the platform while the luggage was being lifted into the car. "We shall have to put the motor up in a day or two. It will not need much of an overhauling in the way of repairs this season, I guess, for it is comparatively new and should be in pretty good condition. There may be a few slight things necessary but nothing much. Isn't that so, Havens?"

"It is badly scratched, sir."

"Scratched!"

"Yes, sir—both inside and out. I wonder you haven't noticed it. Still you wouldn't unless you got it in just the right light. I did not myself at first. There are terrible scratches everywhere. You would think ten men had climbed all over it. Look!"

"Oh, it can't be so bad as all that," laughed Mr. Tolman good-humoredly, evidently not taking the chauffeur's comment seriously. "The car was new in the spring and we have not given it very hard wear. What little luggage we have carried has been carefully put in; I have seen to that myself. Only a short time ago I thought how splendidly fresh the varnish looked. In fact,

I examined it just before you were ill. It can't have become very much defaced since then for we have not had the car out of the garage except for one short excursion."

Havens' brow darkened into a puzzled frown.

"I don't understand it at all, sir," he replied. "I could swear the scratches were not there when I went away. If you didn't tell me yourself the car hadn't been used much I'd stake my oath it had had a great deal of knocking about while I was gone. Look here, Mr. Tolman! Look at that, and that, and that—great digs in the paint as if people with boots on had climbed over the sides."

Mr. Tolman looked and so, with a sinking heart, did Stephen.

"Mercy on us! I never noticed all this before!" cried Mr. Tolman, in consternation. "What in the world—" he stopped as if he could find no words to voice his amazement. "Look at this!" He placed a finger on a broad, clearly defined line that extended from the top of the tonneau to the bottom. "You would think somebody had dug his heels in here and then slid down until he reached the ground! And this! What on earth has happened to the thing, Havens? It looks as if it had been used for a gymnasium."

Hot and cold by turns, Steve listened. The marks to which his father pointed told a truthful story. Somebody had braced his heels against the side and then slid to the ground; it was Bud Taylor. And that other jagged line indicated where Tim Barclay had scrambled over the edge and made his hurried exit. The history of the whole miserable adventure was etched in the varnish as vividly as if it had been traced there in words. Stephen gasped with horror when he saw how plainly the entire story stood out in the sunlight of the November day. Why, the most stupid person alive could read it! Every moment he expected that his father or Havens would wheel on him and ask accusingly:

"When was it you carried all those boys to Torrington?"

He could hear his heart thumping inside him and feel the beat of the blood that scorched his cheek. He had not pictured a dilemma like this. The affair had gone off so smoothly that he had flattered himself every possibility of discovery was past, and in this comforting knowledge he had basked with serenity. And now, behold, here he was at the brink of peril, and just when he had had such a glorious holiday, too!

"How do you solve the riddle, Havens?" he heard his father asking.

"I ain't solvin' it, sir," was the drawling answer. "Maybe Steve could give you a hint, though," he added slyly.

The lad stiffened. He and Havens had never been friends. They had been through too many battles for that. The chauffeur did not like boys and took no trouble to conceal the fact, and as a result he had been the prey of many a mischievous prank. It was through his vigilance that Stephen had more than once been brought to justice and in the punishment that followed Havens had exulted without restraint. As a retaliation the boy tormented him whenever opportunity presented, the two carrying on a half-bitter, half-humorous feud which was a source of mutual gratification.

Had not this been the case the confession that trembled on Stephen's tongue would doubtless have been uttered then and there. But to speak before Havens and afford him the chance to crow and rejoice,—that was not to be thought of. Therefore, drawing in his chin and holding his head a trifle higher than was his wont, he replied with hauteur:

"I've no solution at all to offer. How could I have?"

For the fraction of a second Mr. Tolman looked sharply at

his son as if some new thought had suddenly struck him; then the piercing scrutiny faded from his eyes and he turned away.

"Well, I guess we shall have to drop the matter for the present, anyway, and be getting home," said he. "It will do no good for us to stand here in the cold and argue. We shall be no nearer an answer. Come, jump in, Steve!"

With a strange sense of reluctance the boy obeyed. He felt the door to confession closing with finality behind him; and now that he saw all chance for dallying on its threshold cut off, he began to regret that it should so completely close. Once again the opportunity to clear his conscience had come about in an easy, natural manner; confession had been gently and tactfully invited and he had turned his back. Never again, probably, would he have such a chance as this. Without any ignominious preamble he could have spoken the few words necessary and been a free man! But alas, he had hesitated too long. His father followed him into the car, banged the door, and they shot homeward.

Perhaps, temporized the lad as they rode along, he would say something when they reached the house. Why wasn't it better anyway to wait until he and his father were quiet and alone? Who could blame him for not wanting to confess his misdemeanors before an audience? His father would understand and forgive his reticence, he was sure. Having lulled his conscience to rest with the assurance of this future reparation he sank back against the cushions and drew the robe closer about him. There was no use in letting the ride be spoiled by worry. He did not need to speak until he got back, and he needn't speak at all if he did not wish to. If no favorable opening occurred, why, he could still remain silent and wait a better chance. He had taken no vow, made no promise; nothing actually bound him to act unless he chose.

It was surprising how his spirits rose with this realization. He even ventured to talk a little and make a joke or two. These overtures received only scant response from his father, however, for Mr. Tolman's brow had settled into a frown and it needed no second glance to assure Stephen that the happenings of the past half-hour had put the elder man very much out of humor. How unfortunate, mused the boy, that this mood should have come upon his father. It would take more than an ordinary measure of courage to approach him now. Why, it would be braving the lions, actually tempting fate to go to him with a confession when he looked like this. Would it not be much wiser to wait?

With a sharp swerve they turned in at the gate and rolled up the long driveway; then the front door burst open and from it issued not only Mrs. Tolman and Doris but with them the girl with the wonderful hair, Jane Harden, whom he had seen at Northampton. A hubbub of greeting ensued and in the interchange of gay conversation all thought of confession was swept from Stephen's mind.

Nor in the days that followed, with their round of skating, hockey, snow-shoeing, and holiday festivities, did the inclination to revert to the follies of the past arise. The big red touring-car was sent away without further allusion to its battered condition and with its departure the last link with the misfortunes that tormented him seemed destroyed. Once, it is true, when he overheard his father telling his mother that the bill for repainting and varnishing the car was going to be very large, his conscience smote him. But what, he argued, could he do? Even were he to come forward now and shoulder the blame it would not reduce the expense of which his father complained. He had no money. Therefore he decided it was better to close his ears and try and forget the entire affair. His father had evidently accepted the calamity with resignation and made up his mind to bear the consequences without further demur. Why not let the matter rest there? At this late date it would be absurd to speak, especially when it could not alter the situation.

In the meantime letters came from Mr. Ackerman and from Dick. The latter was very happy at the New Haven school and was making quite a record for himself, and it was easy to detect between the lines of the steamboat magnate's epistle that he was much gratified by the progress of his protégé. Thanksgiving would soon be here and if the Tolmans still extended their invitation for the holidays the two New Yorkers would be glad to accept it.

"I'll write Ackerman to-day," announced Mr. Tolman at breakfast. "The invitation has hung on Stephen and Dick, and I am glad to say they each have made good. How fine that that little East Side chap should have turned out so well! I don't wonder Ackerman is pleased. Everybody does not get appreciation in return for kindness. I know many a parent whose children repay what is done for them only with sneaking, unworthy conduct and utter ingratitude. Dick may not have been born into prosperity but he is a thoroughbred at heart and it shows in his actions. He is every inch a gentleman."

At the words Stephen's blood tingled.

What would his father think of him if he knew what a mean-spirited coward he was? Well, it was impossible to tell him now. It would upset the whole Thanksgiving party.

CHAPTER XVII

MORE STEAMBOATING

The night before Thanksgiving Mr. Ackerman and Dick arrived at Coventry and it was difficult to believe the change wrought in the New York boy. Not only was his face round, rosy and radiant with happiness but along with a new manliness had stolen a gentler bearing and a courtesy that had not been there when he had set forth to school.

"Why, you must have put on ten pounds, Dick!" cried Mr. Tolman, shaking hands with his young guest after greeting the steamboat magnate.

"It is eleven pounds, sir," laughed Dick. "We have bully eats at school and all you want of them."

The final phrase had a reminiscent ring as if it harked back to a time when three ample meals were a mirage of the imagination.

"Well, I am glad to hear you have done justice to them and encouraged the cook," was Mr. Tolman's jocular reply. "Now while you stay here you must cheer on our cook in the same fashion. If you don't we shall think you like New Haven better."

"I guess there is no danger of that," put in Mr. Ackerman. "Dick seems hollow down to his ankles. There is no filling him up; is there, boy?"

"I couldn't eat that third ice-cream you offered me yesterday," was the humorous retort.

"I hope you've saved some room for to-morrow's dinner," Mrs. Tolman interrupted, "for there will be mince pie and plum pudding and I don't know what not. And then there is the turkey—we ordered an extra large one on purpose."

Dick and Steve exchanged a sheepish grin.

"Well, it is jolly to see you good people," Mr. Tolman declared, as he ushered the visitors into the living room, where a bright fire burned on the hearth. "Our boys have done well, haven't they, Ackerman? I don't know which is to win the scholarship race—the steamboats or the railroads."

"We could compare marks," Stephen suggested.

"That would hardly be fair," Mr. Ackerman objected quickly, "for the steamboats did not start even with the railroads in this contest. Dick has had to put in a lot of hours with a tutor to make up for the work he missed at the beginning of the year. He has been compelled to bone down like a beaver to go ahead with his class; but he has succeeded, haven't you, sonny?"

"I hope I have," was the modest retort.

"Furthermore," went on Mr. Ackerman, "there are other things beside scholarship to be considered in this bargain. We want fine, manly boys as well as wise ones. Conduct counts for a great deal, you know."

Stephen felt himself coloring.

"There have been no black marks on Dick's record thus far. How about yours, Steve?" asked the New York man.

"I—er—no. I haven't had any black marks, either," responded Stephen, with a gulp of shame.

"That is splendid, isn't it!" commented Mr. Ackerman. "I wasn't looking for them. You have too fine a father to be anything but a square boy."

Once more Stephen knew himself to be blushing. If they would only talk about something else!

"Are you going to finish your steamboat story for us while you are here?" inquired he with sudden inspiration.

"Why, I had not thought of doing any steamboating down here," laughed the capitalist. "Rather I came to help the Pilgrims celebrate their first harvest."

"But even they had to come to America by boat," suggested Doris mischievously.

"I admit that," owned the New Yorker. "And what is more, they probably would have come in a steamboat if one had been running at the time."

"What was the first American steamship to cross the Atlantic, Ackerman?" questioned Mr. Tolman when they were all seated before the library fire.

"I suppose the *Savannah* had that distinction," was the reply. "She was built in New York in 1818 to be used as a sailing packet; but she had side wheels and an auxiliary engine, and although she did not make the entire trans-Atlantic distance by steam she did cover a part of it under steam power. Her paddle wheels, it is interesting to note, were so constructed that they could be unshipped and taken aboard when they were not in use, or when the weather was rough. I believe it took her twenty-seven days to make the trip from Savannah to Liverpool and eighty hours of that time she was using her engine. Although she made several trips in safety it was quite a while before the American public was sufficiently convinced of the value of steam to build other steamships. A few small ones appeared in our harbors, it is true, but they came from Norway or England; they made much better records, too, than anything previously known, the *Sirius* crossing in 1838 in nineteen days, and the *Great Western* in fifteen. In the meantime shipbuilders on both sides of the Atlantic were studying the steamboat problem and busy brains in Nova Scotia and on the Clyde were working out an answer to the puzzle. One of the most alert of these brains belonged to Samuel Cunard, the founder of the steamship line that has since become world famous. In May, 1840, through his instrumentality, the *Unicorn* set out from England for Boston arriving in the harbor June third after a voyage of sixteen days. When we reflect that she was a wooden side-wheeler, not much larger than one of our tugboats, we marvel that she ever put in her appearance. Tidings of her proposed trip had already preceded her, and when after much anxious watching she was sighted there was the greatest enthusiasm along the water front, the over-zealous populace who wished to give her a royal welcome setting off a six-pounder in her honor that shattered to atoms most of her stained glass as she tied up at the dock."

His audience laughed.

"You see," continued the capitalist, "the ship came in answer to a circular sent out by our government to various shipbuilders asking bids from swift and reliable boats to carry our mails to England. Cunard immediately saw the commercial advantages of such an opportunity, and not having money enough to back the venture himself the Halifax man went to Scotland where he met Robert Napier, a person who like himself had had wide experience in shipping affairs. Both men were enthusiastic over the project; before long the money necessary for the undertaking was raised, and the British and North American Royal Mail Steam Packet Company, with a line of four ships, was awarded the United States Government contract. These ships were very significantly named: the *Britannia* in honor of England, the *Arcadia* as a compliment to Mr. Cunard's Nova Scotia home, the *Caledonia* in memory of Napier's Scotch ancestry, and the *Columbia* out of regard to America. And in passing it is rather interesting to recall that in homage to these pioneer ships it has become a tradition of the Cunard Line to use names that terminate in the letter *a* for all the ships that have followed them. For, you must remember, it was this modest group of steam packets that were the ancestors of such magnificent boats as the *Mauretania* and *Lusitania*."

"There was some difference!" interrupted Stephen.

"Well, rather! Had you, however, told Samuel Cunard then that such mammoth floating hotels were possible he would probably not have believed you. He had task enough on his hands to carry the mails; transport the few venturesome souls that dared to cross the sea; and compete with the many rival steamship lines that sprang up on both sides of the ocean as soon as some one had demonstrated that trans-Atlantic travel was practical. For after Cunard had blazed the path there were plenty of less daring persons ready to steal from him the fruits of his vision and courage. From 1847 to 1857 the Ocean Steamship Company carried mails between New York and Bremen, and there was a very popular line that ran from New York to Havre, up to the period of the Civil War. Among the individual ships none, perhaps, was more celebrated than the *Great Eastern*, a vessel of tremendous length, and one that more nearly approached our present-day liners as to size. Then there was the Collins Line that openly competed with the Cunard Line; and to further increase trans-Atlantic travel, in 1855 Cornelius Vanderbilt, ever at the fore in novel projects, began operating lines of steamships not only to England and France but to Bremen."

Mr. Ackerman paused a moment.

"By 1871 there was an American line between Philadelphia

and Liverpool. In the meantime, ever since 1861, there had been a slow but steady advance in ocean shipbuilding. Although iron ships had gradually replaced wooden ones the side-wheeler was still in vogue, no better method of locomotion having been discovered. When the change from this primitive device to the screw propeller came it was a veritable leap in naval architecture. Now revolutions in any direction seldom receive a welcome and just as the conservatives had at first hooted down the idea of iron ships, asserting they would never float, so they now decried the use of the screw propeller. Indeed there was no denying that this innovation presented to shipbuilders a multitude of new and balking problems. While the clipper ships had greatly improved the designs of vessels the stern was still their weakest point and now, in addition to this already existing difficulty, came the new conundrums presented by the pitch, or full turn of the thread, in the screw propeller; also the churning of the current produced by the rapidly whirling wheel, which was found to retard the speed of the ship very materially. Valiantly engineers wrestled with one after another of these enigmas until they conquered them and put shipbuilding on the upward path where it has been ever since. In time steel ships replaced the cruder vessels of iron; finer types of engines were worked out; the wireless and the many electrical devices which herald approaching foes and announce the presence of icebergs have been invented; until now the ocean liner is practically safe from all perils except fogs, icebergs and submarines."

He stopped a moment with eyes fixed on the glowing logs that crackled on the hearth.

"Meanwhile," he went on, "comfort aboard ship has progressed to luxury. Better systems of ventilation, more roomy sleeping quarters, more windows and improved lighting facilities have been installed. The general arrangement of the ship has also been vastly improved since the days when the high bulwark and long deckhouse were in use. Now iron railings allow the sea to wash back and forth in time of storm, and in consequence there is less danger of vessels being swamped by the waves. Then there are watertight doors and bulkheads, double bottoms to the hulls, and along with these more practical advances have come others of a more healthful and artistic trend. The furniture is better; the decoration of the cabins and saloons prettier and more harmonious; there has been more hygienic sanitation. When the *Oceanic* of the White Star Line was built in 1870 she had a second deck, and this novel feature was adopted broadcast and eventually ushered in the many-deck liners now in use. The *Servia*, built in 1881, was the first steel ship and the advantage of its greater elasticity was instantly seen. Builders were wise enough to grasp the fact that with the increasing length of vessels steel ships would be able to stand a greater strain. Little by little the gain went on in every direction. Nevertheless, in spite of the intelligence of the shipbuilders, it was long before trans-Atlantic navigators had the courage to trust themselves entirely to their engines and discard masts; although they shifted to steel ones instead of those of iron or wood, they still persisted in carrying them."

He smiled as he spoke.

"When the twin-screw propeller made its appearance it brought with it greater speed and there was a revival of the old racing spirit. Between the various shipping lines of all nations the contest for size and swiftness has raged ever since. Before the Great War, Germany had a very extensive collection of large and rapid liners, many of them built on the Clyde, that fought to surpass the Cunard ships. The White Star Line also took a hand in the game and built others. In the contest, alas, America has been far behind until gradually she has let other countries slip in and usurp the major proportion of ocean commerce. It is a pitiful thing that we should not have applied our skill and wealth of material to building fine American steamship lines of our own instead of letting so many of our tourists turn their patronage to ships of foreign nations. Perhaps if the public were not so eager for novelty, and so constantly in search for the newest, the largest and the fastest boats, we should be content to make our crossings in the older and less gaudy ships, which after all are quite as seaworthy. But we Americans must always have the superlative, and therefore many a steamer has had to be scrapped simply because it had no palm gardens, no swimming pools, no shore luxuries. We have not, however, wholly neglected naval construction for we have many fine steamships, a praiseworthy lot of battleships and cruisers and some very fine submarines. I hope and believe that the time will come when our merchant marine will once again stand at the front as it did in the days of the clipper ships. Our commerce reaches out to every corner of the earth and why should we rely on other countries to transport our goods?"

"I suppose there are no pirates now, are there, Mr. Ackerman?" asked Dick, raising his eyes expectantly to the capitalist's face.

"I am afraid there are very few, Dick boy," returned the elder man kindly. "I suppose that is somewhat of a disappointment to you. You would have preferred to sail the seas in the days when every small liner carried her guns as a defence against raiders and was often forced to use them, too. But when international law began to regulate traffic on the high seas and the ocean thoroughfare ceased to be such a deserted one pirates went out of fashion, and every nation was granted equal rights to sail the seas unmolested. It was because this freedom was menaced by German submarines in the late war and our privilege to travel by water threatened that our nation refused to tolerate such conditions. A code of humane laws that had been established for the universal good was being broken and we could not permit it. For you must remember that now there are almost as many laws on the ocean as on the land. There are rules for all kinds of vessels, of which there are a far greater variety than perhaps you realize. Not only have we steamships, cruisers, and battleships but we have schooners, barques, brigs, tugboats, dredgers, oil-tankers, turret ships for freight, cargo boats, steam tramps, coalers, produce ships, ice-breakers, train ferries, steam trawlers, fire boats, river boats, harbor excursion boats, coasters, whalebacks, steam yachts, launches and lake steamers. Each of these is carefully classified and has its particular traffic rules, and in addition to these is obliged to obey certain other general marine laws to which all of them are subject, in order that travel by water may be made safe."

"Don't all ships have to be inspected, too?" asked Stephen.

"Yes; and not only are they inspected but to protect the lives of their passengers and crew, as well as preserve their cargo, they must adhere to specified conditions. The number of passengers and crew is regulated by law, as is the amount of the cargo. Ocean liners, for example, must have aboard a certain number of lifeboats, rafts, belts, life preservers, fire extinguishers, lines of hose; and the size of all these is carefully designated. There must be frequent drills in manning the boats; the fire hose must be tested to see that it works and is in proper condition; and in thick weather the foghorns must be sounded at regular intervals. There is no such thing now as going to sea in haphazard fashion and trusting to luck. Everything that can be done for the safety of those who travel the ocean must be done."

He paused a moment, then added:

"And in the meanwhile, that every protection possible shall be offered to ships, we have been as busy on the land as on the water and have established a code of laws to govern our coasts, harbors and rivers. Government surveys have charted the shores of all countries so that now there are complete maps that give not only the coast line but also the outlying islands, rocks and shoals that might be a menace to ships. It is no longer possible for a State bordering on the sea to put up a low building at the water's edge and set a few candles in the windows as was done back in the year eighteen hundred."

Both the boys laughed.

"We can laugh now," assented Mr. Ackerman with a smile, "but in those days I fancy it was no laughing matter. Even with all our up-to-date devices there are wrecks; and think of the ships that must have gone down before charts were available, lighthouses and bell buoys in vogue, wireless signals invented and the coast patrol in operation. I shudder to picture it. Sailing the seas was a perilous undertaking then, I assure you. Even the first devices for safety were primitive. The Argand lamp of 1812 was not at all powerful and the lenses used were far from perfect. Foghorns were operated by hand or by horse power and were not strong enough to be heard at any great distance. Bell buoys were unknown although there were such things as bell-boats which were anchored in dangerous spots and rung by the wash of the waves. There were lightships, too, but more often than not their feeble light was obscured or unnoticed and they were run down by the ships they sought to protect. Altogether there was room for improvement at every point and slowly but surely it came. After the Daboll trumpet, whistle and siren had been tried, finer horns operated by steam or power engines supplanted them until now all along our coasts and inland streams signals of specified strength have been installed, a commission deciding just what size signals shall be used and where they shall be placed. There are lighthouses of prescribed candle power; automatic flashlights and whistling buoys; coastguard stations with carefully drilled crews; all regulated by law and matters of compulsion. If men and ships are lost now it is because it is beyond human power to help it."

"There are facts about the water that are impossible to modify," interrupted Mr. Tolman, "and I suppose we shall never be able wholly to eliminate the dangers growing out of them. There are for example silence zones where, because of the nature of air currents or atmospheric conditions, no sounds can be heard. Often a foghorn comparatively near at hand will belch forth its warning and its voice be swallowed up in this strange stillness. Many a calamity has occurred that could only be accounted for in this way. Man is ingenious, it is true, but he is not omniscient and in the face of some of the caprices of nature he is powerless."

Mr. Ackerman rose and stood with his back to the fire.

"And now," went on Mr. Tolman, addressing Stephen and Dick, "I should say you two had had quite a lecture on steamboating and should move that you both go to bed."

Quickly Mr. Ackerman interrupted him.

"I should amend the motion by suggesting that we all go to bed," laughed he. "I am quite as tired as the boys are."

The amendment was passed, the motion carried, and soon the entire Tolman family was wrapped in sleep.

CHAPTER XVIII

A THANKSGIVING TRAGEDY

Perhaps had Stephen known what was in store for him on the morrow he might not have slept so soundly. As it was, he and Dick had to be called three times before they opened their eyes on the Thanksgiving sunshine. A heavy frost had fallen during the night, touching the trees with splendor and transforming the brown earth to a jewelled sweep of gems that flashed like brilliants in the golden light. The boys scrambled into their clothes and, ruddy from a cold shower, descended to the dining room where amid the fragrance of steaming coffee the family were just sitting down to breakfast.

"Well, what is up for to-day, boys?" inquired Mrs. Tolman, after the more formal greetings were over. "What are you planning to do with Dick, Stephen?"

"We're going skating over to the Hollow if the ice is any good," was the prompt response. "It was fine yesterday and unless somebody has smashed it all up it ought to be good to-day."

"That plan sounds rather nice, doesn't it, Jane?" Doris suggested to her roommate. "Why don't we go, too?"

"I'd like nothing better," was the answer.

"The youngsters have sketched a very alluring program," Mr. Ackerman said. "If I had any skates I should be tempted to join them. I have not been on the ice in years but in my day I used to be quite a hockey player."

"Oh, do come, Mr. Ackerman!" cried Steve eagerly. "If you used to skate it will all come back to you. It is like swimming, you know; once you have learned you never forget how."

"But I've nothing to skate with," laughed the New Yorker.

"Oh, we can fix you up with skates all right, if you really want to go," Mr. Tolman said. "I have a couple of pairs and am sure you could manage to use one of them."

"So you are a skater, are you, Tolman?" the capitalist observed, with surprise.

"Oh, I am nothing great," Mr. Tolman protested, "but I have always enjoyed sports and muddled along at them. Coventry is quite a distance from Broadway, you see, and therefore we must get our recreation in other ways."

"It is a darn sight better than anything New York has to offer," commented the other man soberly. "Good wholesome out-of-door exercise is not to be mentioned in the same breath with a hot theater where a picture show is a makeshift for something better. Give me fresh air and exercise every time!"

"Well, since that is the way you feel about it we can comply with your request," Mr. Tolman rejoined, with a smile. "If you do not mind hobbling back to New York lame as a cart-horse you can certainly have your wish, for we have the ice, the skates, plenty of coats and sweaters—everything necessary. Suppose we all start for the Hollow at ten o'clock. It is a mile walk but as we are having a late dinner we shall still have a long morning."

"That will suit me all right," returned Mr. Ackerman.

"By the way, Henry," interrupted Mrs. Tolman, addressing her husband, "Havens is waiting to see you. He has some message for you."

"Where is he?"

"In the hall."

"Ask Mary to tell him to go into my den. I'll be there in a minute."

What a merry party it was that chatted and laughed there in the warmth of the sunny dining room! For the time being the elders dropped their cares and became as young in spirit as the boys and girls. Jokes, stories and good-humored banter passed back and forth until with one accord everybody rose from the table and sauntered into the library where a great blaze of logs glowed and crackled.

"If you will excuse me I will see what Havens wants," remarked Mr. Tolman, as he lighted his cigar. "Probably the garage people have unearthed some more repairs that must be made on that car. They seem to have a faculty for that sort of thing. Every day they discover something new the matter with it. I shall have a nice little bill by the time they finish."

Shrugging his shoulders, he passed into the hall. It was more than half an hour before he returned and when he did a close observer would have noticed that his face had lost its brightness and that the gaiety with which he took up the conversation with his guests was forced and unnatural. However, he tried resolutely to banish his irritation, whatever its cause. He went up to the attic with Mr. Ackerman, where the two searched out skates, woolen gloves and sweaters; he jested with Doris and Jane Harden; he challenged Dick to a race across the frozen ground. But beneath his lightness lingered a grave depression which betokened to those who knew him best that something was wrong. Yet he was evidently determined the cloud should not obtrude itself and spoil the happiness of the day. Probably some business annoyance that could not be remedied had arisen;

or possibly Havens had given notice. Such contingencies were of course to be deplored but as they could not be helped, why let them ruin the entire holiday?

Therefore nobody heeded Mr. Tolman's mood which was so well controlled that his guests were unconscious of it, and the group of skaters swung along over the frosty fields with undiminished merriment. The Hollow for which they were bound lay in a deserted stone quarry where a little arm of the river had penetrated the barrier of rocks and, gradually flooding the place, made at one end a deep pool; from this point the water spread itself over the meadows in a large, shallow pond. Had the spot been nearer the town it would doubtless have been overrun with skaters; but as it was isolated, and there was a larger lake near the center of the village, few persons took the trouble to seek out this remote stretch of ice.

This morning it lay desolate like a gleaming mirror, not a human being marring its solitude.

"We shall have the place all to ourselves!" exclaimed Mr. Ackerman. "There will be no spectators to watch me renew my youth, thank goodness!"

Quickly the skates were strapped on and the young people shot out into the sunshine and began to circle about. More cautiously Mr. Tolman and his guest followed.

"I wouldn't go into the quarry," shouted Mr. Tolman, "for I doubt if it has been cold enough yet to freeze the ice very solidly there. There are liable to be air holes where the river makes in."

"Oh, we fellows have skated in the quarry millions of times, Dad," Stephen protested. "It is perfectly safe."

"There is no way of telling whether it is or not," was the response, "so suppose for to-day we keep away from it."

"But—"

"Oh, don't argue, Stevie," called Doris. "If Dad doesn't want us to go there that's enough, isn't it?"

"But half the fun is making that turn around the rocks," grumbled Stephen, in a lower tone. "I don't see why Dad is such a fraid-cat. I know this pond better than he does and—"

"If your father says not to skate there that ought to go with you," cut in Dick. "He doesn't want you to—see? Whether it is safe or not has nothing to do with it."

"But it's so silly!" went on Stephen. "Why—"

"Oh, cut it out! Can it!" ejaculated the East Side lad. "Your dad says *No* and he's the boss."

The ungracious retort Steve offered was lost amid the babel of laughter that followed, and the skaters darted away up the pond. Indeed, one could not long have cherished ill humor amid such radiant surroundings. There was too much sunshine, too much sparkle in the clear air; too much jollity and happiness. Almost before he realized it Stephen's irritation had vanished and he was speeding across the glassy surface of the ice as gay as the gayest of the company.

He never could explain afterward just how it happened that he found himself around the bend of the quarry and sweeping with the wind toward its farther end. He had not actually formulated the intention of slipping away from the others and invading this forbidden spot. Nevertheless, there he was alone in the tiny cove with no one in sight. What followed was all over in a moment,—the breaking ice and the plunge into the frigid water. The next he knew he was fighting with all his strength to prevent himself from being drawn beneath the jagged, crumbling edge of the hole. To clamber out was impossible, for every time he tried the thin ice would break afresh under his hands and submerge him again in the bitter cold of the mov-

HE WAS FIGHTING TO PREVENT HIMSELF FROM BEING DRAWN
BENEATH THE JAGGED, CRUMBLING EDGE OF THE HOLE.

ing stream. Over and over he tried to pull himself to safety but without success. Then suddenly he felt himself becoming numb and helpless. His teeth chattered and he could no longer retain his hold on the frail support that was keeping his head above water. He was slipping back into the river. *He was not going to be able to get out!*

With a piercing scream he made one last desperate lunge forward, and again the ice that held him broke and the water dashed over his ears and mouth.

When he next opened his eyes it was to find himself in his own bed with a confusion of faces bending over him.

"There!" he heard some one say in a very small, far-away voice. "He is coming to himself now, thank God! It was chiefly cold and fright. He is safe now, Tolman. Don't you worry! You'd better go and get off some of your wet clothing, or you will catch your death."

Mr. Ackerman was speaking.

"Yes, Henry, do go!" pleaded his wife.

As Stephen looked about him in the vague, groping uncertainty of returning consciousness his glance fell upon his father who stood beside his pillow, shivering nervously. He put out his hand and touched the dripping coat sleeve.

"What—" began he weakly.

Then with a rush it all came back to him and everything was clear. He had been drowning and his father had plunged into the water to save him!

A sob rose in his throat and he caught the elder man's hand between both of his.

"Oh, Dad," he exclaimed, "I've been so rotten to you—so mean—so cowardly. I'm ashamed to—"

"Don't talk about it now, son. I know."

"You know what I did?"

"Yes."

"But—" the boy paused bewildered.

"Don't talk any more about it now, Stevie," pleaded his mother.

"But I've got to know," said the lad. "Can't you see that—"

"Let me talk with him alone a moment," suggested Mr. Tolman in an undertone. "He is all upset and he won't calm down until he has this thing off his mind. Leave me here with him a little while. I'll promise that he does not tire himself."

The doctor, Mr. Ackerman and Mrs. Tolman moved across the room toward the window.

"You asked how I knew, son," began his father with extreme gentleness. "I didn't really know. I just put two and two together. There was the scratched machine and the gasoline gone—both of which facts puzzled me not a little. But the proof that clinched it all and made me certain of what had happened came to me this morning when Havens brought me an old red sweater and some school papers of Bud Taylor's that the men who were overhauling the car found under the seat. In an instant the whole thing was solved."

"You knew before we went skating then?"

"Yes."

"And—and—you jumped into the water after me just the same."

Mr. Tolman's voice trembled:

"You are my son and I love you no matter what you may do."

"Oh, Dad, I'm so sorry!" sobbed the boy. "I wanted to tell you—I meant to. It was just that I was too much of a coward. I was so ashamed of what I had done that I hadn't the nerve. After it was over it all seemed so wrong. I knew you would be angry—"

"Rather say *sorry*, son."

"Well, sorry. And now that you have been so white to me I'm more ashamed still."

"There, there, my boy, we will say no more about it," his father declared. "You and your conscience have probably had a pretty bitter battle and I judge you have not been altogether happy since your adventure. People who do wrong never are. It is no fun to carry your fault to bed with you and find it waiting when you wake up in the morning."

"You bet it isn't!" replied the lad, with fervor. "But can't I do something now to make good, Dad?"

Mr. Tolman checked an impulsive protest and after a moment responded gravely:

"We will see. Perhaps you would like to earn something toward doing over the car."

"Yes! Yes! I would!"

"Well, all that can be arranged later. We—"

"Henry," broke in Mrs. Tolman, "you must go this instant and get into some dry clothes. You are chilled through. The doctor says Stephen is going to be none the worse for his ducking and that he can come down stairs to dinner after he has rested a little longer. So our Thanksgiving party is not to be spoiled, after all. In fact, I believe we shall have more to give thanks for than we expected," concluded she, making an unsteady attempt to speak lightly.

"I think so, too," echoed her husband.

"And so do I!" added Stephen softly, as he exchanged an affectionate smile with his father.

CHAPTER XIX

THE END OF THE HOUSE PARTY

As they were persons of strong constitution and in good athletic training neither Mr. Tolman nor Steve were any the worse for the narrow escape of the morning, and although a trifle spent with excitement both were able to take their places at the dinner table so that no cloud rested on the festivity of the day.

Certainly such a dinner never was,—or if there ever had been one like it in history at least Dick Martin had never had the luck to sit down to it. The soup steaming and hot, the celery white and crisp, the sweet potatoes browned in the oven and gleaming beneath their glaze of sugar, the cranberry sauce vivid as a bowl of rubies; to say nothing of squash, and parsnips and onions! And as for the turkey,—why, it was the size of an ostrich! With what resignation it lay upon its back, with what an abject spirit of surrender,—as if it realized that resistance was futile and that it must docilely offer itself up to make perfect the feast. And the pudding, the golden-tinted pies with their delicate crust, the nuts; the pyramid of fruit, riotous in color; the candies of every imaginable hue and flavor! Was it a wonder that Dick, who had never before beheld a real New England home Thanksgiving, regarded the novelty with eyes as large as saucers and ate until there was not room for another mouthful?

"Gee!" he gasped in a whisper to Stephen, as he sank weakly back into his chair when the coffee made its appearance. "This sure is some dinner."

The others who chanced to overhear the observation laughed.

"Had enough, sonny?" inquired Mr. Tolman.

"Enough!"

There was more laughter.

"I suppose were it not for the trains and the ships we should not be having such a meal as this to-day," remarked Mrs. Tolman.

"You are right," was Mr. Ackerman's reply. "Let me see! Fruit from Florida, California and probably from Italy; flour from the Middle West; coffee from South America; sugar probably from Cuba; turkey from Rhode Island, no doubt; and vegetables from scattered New England farms. Add to this cigarettes from Egypt and Turkey and you have covered quite a portion of the globe."

"It is a pity we do not consider our indebtedness to our neighbors all over the world oftener," commented Mr. Tolman. "We take so much for granted these days. To appreciate our blessings to the full we should have lived in early Colonial times when the arrival of a ship from across the ocean was such an important event that the wares she brought were advertised broadcast. Whenever such a vessel came into port a list of her cargo was issued and purchasers scrambled eagerly to secure the luxuries she carried. Pipes of wine, bolts of cloth, china, silks, tea—all were catalogued. It was no ordinary happening when such a boat docked, I assure you."

"I suppose it was a great event," reflected Mrs. Tolman, "although I never half realized it."

"And not only was the advent of merchandise a red-letter day but so was the advent of travelers from the other side of the water. Picture if you can the excitement that ensued when

Jenny Lind, the famous singer, visited this country! And the fact that we were now to hear this celebrated woman was not the only reason for our interest. She had actually come in a ship from across the sea! Others would come also. America was no longer cut off from the culture of the old world, an isolated country bereft of the advantages of European civilization. We were near enough for distinguished persons to make trips here! Charles Dickens and the Prince of Wales came—and how cosmopolitan we felt to be entertaining guests from the mother-country! Certainly the Atlantic could not be very wide if it could be crossed so easily and if we could have the same speakers, the same readers, the same singers as did the English! Our fathers and grandfathers must have thrilled with satisfaction at the thought. The ocean was conquered and was no longer an estranging barrier."

"What would they have said to crossing the water by aeroplane or bobbing up in a foreign port in a submarine?" put in Doris.

"And some day I suppose the marvels of our age that cause our mouths to open wide and our eyes to bulge with amazement will become as humdrum as the ocean liner and the Pullman have," Mrs. Tolman remarked.

"Yes," returned her husband. "Think of the fight every one of these innovations has had to put up before it battled its way to success. The first locomotives, you remember, were not only rated as unsafe for travel but also actually destructive to property. The major part of the public had no faith in them and predicted they would never be used for general travel. As for crossing the ocean—why, one was welcome to take his life in his hands if he chose, of course; but to cross in an iron ship—it was tempting Providence! Did not iron always sink? And how people ridiculed Darius Green and his flying machine! Most of the prophets were thought to be crazy. History is filled with stories of men who wrecked their worldly fortunes to perpetuate an idea, and but too frequently an idea they never lived to see perfected."

During the pause that followed Mr. Ackerman leaned across the table and as he sipped his coffee asked mischievously:

"Well, Steve, having now heard both stories, have you come to a conclusion which one you are going to vote for?"

"No, sir," was the dubious response. "I'm farther away from a decision than ever. Just as I get it settled in my mind that the railroads have done the biggest things and conquered the most difficulties along come the steamships and I am certain they are six times as wonderful."

"And you, Dick—what do you say?" questioned the financier, smiling. "Surely you are going to stand up for the steamboat."

But to his chagrin Dick shook his head.

"I feel as Steve does," replied he. "No sooner do I get settled one way than something turns me round the other."

"So far as I can see we shall have to leave the matter a draw, shan't we, Tolman?" observed the New Yorker.

"It would be a jolly subject for a debate, wouldn't it?" put in Stephen. "Sometimes we have discussions like that at school and the next time we do I believe I'll suggest this topic. It would be mighty interesting."

"It certainly would," his father echoed. "But it also would be a very sorry event if you could not demonstrate that the railroads had the supremacy for were their prestige to be threatened I might have to move out of town."

"In case Connecticut did not want you, you might come to New York where you would be sure of being appreciated," put in Mr. Ackerman. "And that is not all talk, either, for I want you and the whole family to give me a promise to-day that you will come over and join Dick and me at Christmas. I've never had a boy of my own to celebrate the holiday with before, you must remember; but this time I have a real family and I am going to have a real Christmas," he continued, smiling affectionately at the lad beside him. "So I want every one of you to come and help me to make the day a genuine landmark. And if I'm a little new at playing Santa Claus some of you who have been schooled in the rôle for many years can show me how. We can't promise to stage for you such an excitement as Stephen got up for us this morning, and we never can give you a dinner equal to this; but we can give you a royal welcome. You can come by boat or come by train," added he slyly. "No guest who patronizes the railroads will be shut out, even if he is misguided. The chief thing is for you to come, one and all, and we will renew our friendship and once again bless Stephen, Dick, and my lost pocketbook, for bringing us together."